Pearl
A New Chapter in an Old Story

Pearl

A New Chapter in an Old Story

Joseph E. Scalia

josephescalia.com

Copyright © 2000 by Joseph E. Scalia

ISBN #:   Softcover   1-4010-0045-2
                      978-1-4010-0045-5

All rights reserved. No part of this book may be reproduced or transmitted in any form or by any means, electronic or mechanical, including photocopying, recording, or by any information storage and retrieval system, without permission in writing from the copyright owner.

This is a work of fiction. Names, characters, places and incidents either are the product of the author's imagination, or are used fictitiously, and any resemblance to any actual persons, living or dead, events, or locales is entirely coincidental.
This book was printed in the United States of America

Second Printing

Dedication

for

my father and mother who gave me life,

my sister Beverly who helped me smile again

in the middle of profound sadness,

and for John Steinbeck

who gave me something to teach, to love and to write.

Preface

JOHN STEINBECK'S *NOVELLA The Pearl* (I prefer the smooth sound of the Italian word for a short novel to the harsher sounding "novelette," that sounds more like something you'd smoke between chapters!) is the perfect work of fiction. The book, originally written as a film script, was later revised into a long magazine story and then published in 1947 in its present form. My love and appreciation for the work grew over the years that I taught it, but I was hooked the first time I read it.

Like most junior and senior high school English teachers I had to "sell" the book to my classes *every single year*, just to get them to take it home! "If nothing else," I told them, "it isn't heavy, it's short, and the print is large so it's easy to read." Then to prove my point I read it with them. And I read it, and I read it, again and again, every year, with every class, for more than twenty-five years. It never got old! What I learned from reading this story (that sounds more like poetry, even though it doesn't rhyme!) is that *I* learned something new every time I read it. Although it seems deceptively simple at first, there is a depth and universality in Steinbeck's story that taps into the human experience of good and evil. It is tightly woven, and without a single extraneous word.

In 1995, I had the opportunity to write for the Research & Education Association (REA) when they launched their Max Notes® Series of review books, an attempt to compete with Cliffs Notes®. I authored two, for Shakespeare's *Julius Caesar* and George Orwell's *Animal Farm,* and I co-wrote one, for Steinbeck's *Of Mice and Men.* In the process, my research revealed much information about the man and more about *The Pearl.*

While Steinbeck was collecting marine specimens from the Gulf of California with his long-time friend, Ed Rickets, he also gathered material that, in 1941, became his first non-fiction book, *The Sea of Cortez*. That, according to his account, was when Steinbeck heard the true story of a young Indian's discovery of "The Pearl of the World," that formed the basis for *The Pearl*, published some six years later. Ironically, Steinbeck learned, the man's good fortune, a seeming assurance of physical and spiritual security, brought him only misfortune and disaster. The incident ended with the young Indian losing what little he had, and throwing his pearl away. Steinbeck refined the "folk tale," which he said, "sounded like a story even though it was probably true." He gave the young Indian a wife and a child, and he honed it to perfection into a work of fiction that just *had* to be true.

From the beginning I approached *The Pearl* as a story of oppression, injustice and reluctant revolution. I always began my introduction with a poorly drawn map on the blackboard and a sketchy history lesson about Cortez, Christianity, horses, gunpowder, and their impact on the Aztecs in the 1500s. If nothing else it gave them a new understanding of "Montezuma's Revenge" that went beyond the possible effects of eating Mexican food and drinking the local water while on vacation there. With each new "teaching" I hoped to get the classes to see why it was so bad for a doctor to withheld his skills from people who couldn't pay, to recognize the evils of a system where pearl buyers are a monopoly and fix their prices to keep poor Indians poor, and to comprehend how a priest wielding the power of eternal salvation or damnation is the most dangerous of all.

One year, to make the situation faced by Steinbeck's characters "realer" to my classes, I invented a board game that I called *Beat the System*. Loosely based on Monopoly®, I purposely made it impossible for them to win. The game divided everybody in the class into different "families," all vying against each other to earn enough money to survive, pay for food, shelter, maybe a couple of luxuries, and to cope with the unexpected problems, disasters and catastrophes that came on practically every roll of the dice. Then, to make family matters worse, there were fees, transaction costs and taxes tacked on to *every* procedure. And I, acting as the bank, the government or the hand of God, always took a cut!

On the appointed day of the playing, I invited my principal (A) so he could get in his yearly mandatory observation, and (B) so he could marvel at my "creative innovation and overall genius." The class did its part, performing beyond even my greatest expectations. Family members skulked around stealing from other families. They all cheated. They all lied. And one family group even resorted to counterfeiting paper money I had printed in their desperate attempt to win a game that was rigged against them from the start. That year my classes read *The Pearl* with the greater insight that they had gained from the lessons they learned by their personal experience trying to *Beat the System.*

In the post-observation conference, my principal's only comment was: "They were all out of their seats!"

An examination of the main characters in *The Pearl* according to modern standards revealed them to be victims, not only of the corrupt system intent on perpetuating itself by keeping them down, but also of their own genders, as Steinbeck presented them. It was easy to see that Kino has no choice *but* to behave always as a man is expected to behave. His actions are motivated by pride. He must prove his courage, be true to his word, and *never* back down, much like, I pointed out, the ever-fighting 9th grade boys that I taught! And Juana, with the one exception when she stands up to her husband, is always the subservient woman and dutiful wife, as she should be. That observation wasn't very popular with the girls. It made the boys puff up. And a mini battle of the sexes erupted. So I decided on an object lesson and waited the perfect occasion to deliver it.

Home Economic Class was once where the girls at the junior high learned how to sew and make things. Shop Class was where the boys, in the process of making bookracks or ashtrays, learned how to cut their fingers off on the electric saws. Today, in the interest of "equality," Home Ec and Shop have been combined and renamed "Home and Careers," because both girls and boys now have to take the same class. Back then, the Home Economics Department sponsored "Skirt Day" every year as an opportunity to show off the sewing skills their girls had learned in class. For a week before the big event the signs posted all around the school proclaimed: "Thursday is Skirt Day!" And they encouraged: "Everybody wear a skirt!"

So I did.

It was a gray wrap-around that I had borrowed for the occasion, the perfect complement to my construction boots and white athletic socks. When the bell rang I put it on over my rolled up my Levis and headed into the hall toward class. It didn't take long for word to get around the building, and in less than a minute an assistant principal scurried down to the Main Office with the news, "Scalia's wearing a skirt!" In less time than that I saw the same "out of their seats" principal, now purple-faced, heading in my direction. Several minutes later I was seated in his office with my legs delicately crossed and my skirt modestly pulled down over my knees. Of course he was outraged by my display and demanded an explanation. I pointed out to him that I was only following the directions that had asked *everyone* to wear a skirt on Skirt Day. I also added that I was teaching a lesson on "sex stereotyping and sex discrimination," and that his negative attitude was proving my point. In the end we reached a compromise -- I agreed not to wear my skirt *in* the halls, and he grudgingly consented that I could wear it *in* class. Within minutes I was back in front of the classroom, skirted, and the lesson on sexism was one my classes would never forget. To this day there are students, whose mothers or fathers were in my class that year, who ask me about the time I wore a dress to school! And for the record, that was the last "Skirt Day" the school ever had.

Another time, to prove how trusting people might be easily misled, and explain why Kino, who in the words of the class was "so stupid that he allowed himself to be so easily tricked," I got all of my students to wear decorated paper bags on their heads, in class, *for a whole week!* I accomplished it with the promise of giving everyone who wore a paper bag hat a hundred every day they did, and a bonus hundred for the winner of "Best Hat Competition" at the end of the week. I even got them to parade around the room modeling their work. Seeing all those "cool" fourteen-year-olds sitting there, day after day, in their homemade, individually personalized paper hats, it was difficult for me to keep a straight face. But I did. In the end, of course, I erased all those hundreds, denied everything I had said, and they had a firsthand demonstration of how even such "sophisticates" as they might be cheated.

I mention all this to illustrate just how much I loved teaching *The Pearl*, and the great lengths I was prepared to go to get my students involved.

My novel, *Pearl*, came about by accident, after my 9th Grade English Honors students asked if we could "do something interesting for a change." So I scrapped the unit test I had planned and I asked them to write a story instead. Which, in their collective opinion, wasn't much better than a unit test. I told them to use *The Pearl* as a jumping off point, and to pick a setting and a time -- before Steinbeck's plot began, while it was going on, or after it ended. They could use his characters, invent their own, or a combination of ingredients. And then they had to write a new chapter to the old story. Of course they complained, but I told them that I'd even write my own chapter, and on the day it was due we shared what we had created. Once again the results exceeded my expectations.

It was Ross F, Alia A's nemesis and chief rival, a student in the truest sense of the word, and quite a writer himself, who became my teacher that day. "Hey," he said after I'd read my chapter to the class, "that's pretty good. You should think about writing a book."

A light bulb lit over my head. For years I had been telling those who complained they didn't have anything to write about: "Write about what you love, about what you know best!" And what better for *me* to write about than something I loved, had been teaching for years, and knew better than the names of my own four kids! That night I went home and added a second chapter, which I also shared with the class. I worked on the story over time and it took me three years to finish. So, what started out as a lark, a tribute to Steinbeck, a way to avoid grading another batch of boring tests, turned into a real book. By then Ross was a senior, one of the best writers in my Creative Writing, and the first one to read the finished, but unedited manuscript.

Although I wrote *Pearl* in a conscious effort to emulate Steinbeck's voice and tone, it is not intended to be a lesser imitation of his greater work. *Pearl* does *not* depend on a pre-reading of Steinbeck's masterpiece, however, doing so will help the reader to understand my use of language and style that I have attempted to carry over. The setting is the same, La Paz, a city on Mexico's Baja Peninsula, which has been at the center of pearl fishing since long before the Spanish arrived. It is highly unlikely that the pearl in my book is the same one that was thrown back into the water at the end of Steinbeck's. I have to admit that my knowledge of pearls is based entirely on what I read in Chapter Two of *The Pearl*, and what I learned, between naps, from a steady diet of PBS specials on the cultured pearl industry in Japan. But even if a pearl has the staying power of a diamond, it's doubtful that one could survive underwater for such a long period of time. However, the prospect that it *might* be the same, as I have hinted, is another attempt, unrealistic though it may be, to further connect both stories. I have endeavored to make the characters of Lucio and Corina, like Kino and Juana in Steinbeck's work, and Shakespeare's Romeo and Juliet, easy to identify with for junior and senior high school students. And because I provide such little description, the readers can visualize them however they choose to do so. My story is intended to stand on its own, to be read, and to be judged on its own merits.

In 1947, John Steinbeck put the town of La Paz on the map with publication of *The Pearl*. In 1977, Scott O'Dell's original novel *Black Pearl* brought readers back to La Paz for another look. Today my *Pearl* takes up where both stories left off. Nearly a century after his grandfather Kino's ordeal, little has changed in the Mexican town, and less for Lucio, the pearl fisherman, that is, until he finds a wonderful pearl, and all of his dreams seem about to come true.

Who knows, perhaps this "New Chapter in an Old Story" will someday become the subject of classroom discussions in the new century!

Joseph E. Scalia -- February 2001

Other books by the author:

FREAKs (Xlibris ISBN 0-7388-3511-0 or 978-0-7388-3511-2)

No Strings Attached (Publish America ISBN 1-4137-0549-9 or 978-1-4137-0549-2)

Brooklyn Family Scenes (Tawny Girl Press ISBN 978-1-60402-882-9)

Scalia vs. The Universe Or: My Life And Hard Times (Tawny Girl Press ISBN 978-1-6042-883-6)

"And Kino drew back his arm and flung the pearl with all his might. Kino and Juana watched it go, winking and glimmering under the setting sun. They saw the little splash in the distance, and they stood side by side watching the place for a long time."

John Steinbeck

from *The Pearl*, 1947

Chapter One

Lucio lived in the cluster of dusty shacks and metal Quonset huts on the outskirts of La Paz. For generations his people had lived, and worked, and died here. Rarely did a person born in this little Mexican village ever leave it, or even travel very far. This was the only home they ever knew for their entire life, and it was the world to them.

Although the people were not all related by blood in a family sense, they were bound together by the blood that they spilled in the daily struggles to survive. And it was this that brought them even closer than any family. By chance they were thrown together, but of necessity they were united – against the tantrums of nature manifested in the violent storms that sometimes blew out of the Sea of Cortez, now called the Gulf of California. Periodically, as though willed by the vengeful gods, the winds ripped through the estuary, destroying the houses fashioned from rusted metal and corrugated tin, the rough wooden shacks made from packing crates, and left the people who had so little without homes. With great determination they battled the sea that was at once their friend, providing them with life and their enemy, often taking away the very lives of so many of these poor fishers.

Together the people of La Paz celebrated life. They rejoiced in the marriages of their young, and were hopeful with the birth of each new child. And together they mourned, for they were no strangers to Death. Death was something that came and found them much too easily, often assuming the guise of accident and chance. Death was a figure that hovered in the dark corners of a room, who came to them in the form of sickness, starvation and in childbirth, or from the stinging bite of a snake. Death was a silent passenger who daily rode with them in their fishing boats, or appeared suddenly in the violent Gulf storms. Death waited in the jaws of the sharks that threatened their fragile lives forty feet below the surface of the blue waters, where the fishers dived for pearls. There, with only as much air as a man could hold in his lungs and a diving knife for protection, a pearl fisher struggled to tear Luck loose with the oysters that clung to the coral reefs. And because Death was always so near, the people weren't afraid, but they had learned to accept Death with resigned indifference, as the inevitable and sometimes welcome conclusion to a hard life.

Then it was the tearful women of the village who carefully washed and wrapped the dead, preparing them for burial. It was the stoical men who carried their dead to the sacred ground of the cemetery behind the large church. And the tired old priest sprinkled holy water with indifference on the crude wooden coffins, and said his mumbled magic prayers that liberated their souls and elevated them to a better, easier eternal life.

Luck was something real and important to these people, as real to them as their religion, a curious blend of Christianity mingled with the old Indian beliefs from the time before the strangers came to change their lives forever. To them, Luck was as tangible and palpable as the Christian God who lived inside their church. So daily the people prayed to the infant Jesus to send Luck on a visit whenever they marked their numbers for the lottery. They lit candles and recited their magic spells to coax the crucified Christ to move God the Father and the other ancient gods to send Luck to the sandy floor of the Gulf whenever they dived for pearls. This trinity of Luck, Religion and Superstition was second only to the Father, Son and Holy Ghost. It colored every facet of the people's being, and it gave meaning to their difficult lives. But even if the gods refused their requests for fortune, the people still prayed for Luck, for they knew that often it was only by courting Luck that Death could be avoided.

And in their deepest desperation, the people of La Paz always maintained their impossible dreams, and their fervent hopes. They said their prayers of being some day blessed, of finding a pearl that might give some comfort to their difficult lives and change them for the better. And because this was the way of life in La Paz, it was also how these people viewed the world.

Lucio was just one fisherman in La Paz. He was a young man, strong, and dependable. Everyone in the village knew that he was someone to be counted on whenever there was hard work to be done, whenever there was the need of another pair of hands, or a strong back. And Lucio was handsome too. In the day time, when he wandered by the houses of his neighbors on his way to the beach, or into the city to sell his pearls to the buyers, all the little girls giggled and called to him when he passed, "Good morning, Lucio." "How are you today, Lucio?"

The young women, who were more reserved, smiled shyly if they caught his glance, or they hid their faces behind lace shawls as he went by them, and they blushed behind their hands to cover their embarrassment that Lucio might be able to read their secret thoughts from their eyes. Often at nighttime under the security of darkness, when the only sounds were those of sleep, it was Lucio who entered the dreams of these same young women. So now when they saw him pass in the daylight it made them blush even more.

But as Lucio walked by he always held his head high and kept his eyes focused straight ahead. This was done not out of any sense of pride or conceit, but out of innocence. For Lucio was a simple man who never considered what effect he might have on the hearts of these young daughters of his neighbors. He did not give this matter a single thought, as he hardly gave a thought to any of those who always thought of him.

However, there was one young woman, Corina, the only daughter of Ernesto and Heléna, who was special to him. When they were children he took an interest in Corina and protected her when they played together. Then, when he was older and had to give up being a child to learn fishing with his father, Lucio often looked for her on the beach where she remained with the other young girls. And Corina watched Lucio as well, worrying him safely home on stormy days, waiting for his boat to return.

After the death of Lucio's father, whose life was taken by the sharks in a dive for pearls, and after the death of his mother from her sorrow, Lucio was alone in the world. Then it was Ernesto who became like his second father, completing Lucio's education, teaching him the secrets that would enable him to hold his breath just a little longer to take more oysters on every dive. And it was Ernesto's wife Heléna and their budding flower, Corina, who brought Lucio food to keep up his strength, and provided some solace for his sorrow, until he was able to deal with his great loss.

It was no wonder that this same girl, Corina, having grown into a beautiful young woman, who often found her way into Lucio's secret thoughts and into his plans for the future. He knew that some day, when he picked someone to marry, it would be no one but Corina, if she would have him. But Lucio also knew that marriage could come only when he had the money to support a wife and the means to provide for the children that would inevitably follow.

So, for the present, Lucio put the thought of Corina and the dream of marriage in the back of his mind. And although he felt the occasional loneliness of a bachelor, and sometimes he yearned for the warmth and softness of a wife who would comfort his nights, Lucio was glad most often that the only worries that filled his head were for his own survival, and for the illusive pearls that he hunted. For the present, at least, his only concern had to be for himself.

Like the other pearl fishers, Lucio prayed to Our Lady of Loreto, the Virgin Mother of the Christ Child, to intercede on his behalf with her Son for the good fortune to find just one pearl to change his life. Sometimes, before a dive Lucio threatened and sometimes he pleaded directly with God the Father, and with all his ancient gods, bargaining with them for good luck. Lucio made a solemn promise that if his prayers were answered he would tithe and donate a tenth of his fortune to the church in La Paz, and that he would make generous contributions to the poor as well. Lucio knew that this was just a fancy, as remote a chance as picking the winning numbers in the national lottery. But there was a part of him that secretly believed it could all come to pass, and that thought gave Lucio some hope.

La Paz was known for the beauty of its pearls, collected and used by the Aztec artisans in their work even before Columbus arrived in the New World more than five hundred years ago. When the plunderers came over the blue water in their floating houses, with their horses and their gunpowder and their new religion, they were at first welcomed as gods. And in return these gods conquered the people who greeted them with open arms. They stripped the Gulf of its treasure, sending back in their strange wooden ships great fortunes of gold, silver and pearls to adorn the robes of Spanish kings, of European nobles, and of Catholic popes. The gold and silver were pure and the price of pearls gathered at the cost of the Indian lives, which were expendable, was cheap. For centuries the strangers enslaved and exploited these people and dominated the land and sea.

But even after the stranglehold of Spanish colonialism was broken, the next onslaught that swept south along the *Baja* into La Paz came from corrupt government officials in far away Mexico City. And nothing changed for the pearl fishers, except the faces of the strangers who lined their pockets with wealth and almost depleted what remained of the pearls.

In the last remaining years of the 20th Century, the invasion came in the form of big North *Americano* petroleum companies in search of cheap oil to fuel the fancy cars of *gringos* in the U.S. They were followed by a flood of manufacturers eager for cheap laborers to assemble their machines or sew their labels on clothing and sneakers that would sell for a fortune in the North. Prosperity came to the *Baja*, as up and down the coast mechanical monsters drilled the sea and tore up the land. But it was prosperity only for the strangers, for those who owned the factories. The vacation homes, the new condominiums were built for the *gringo* businessmen who ran these factories and needed places to escape the pressures of their lives. It was prosperity as well for the officials in

Mexico City, eager to line their pockets with easy money and bribes. They passed the laws to protect these new *conquistadors*, again handing over land they didn't own and sacrificing the lives of people they didn't know. And La Paz became the new Mecca for hordes of speculators who, like Midas, hoped to turn cheap land into gold. Soon vacationing *gringos* clogged the barren streets, fast food chains mushroomed beside the quaint silver and pottery shops, and the once pure waters of the Gulf filled with dead fish and pollution. Foul oil and gasoline from industrial spills and the many pleasure boats that put into the estuary smothered the young oysters in their beds and threatened to destroy all that once had been. Now Lucio and his people, even in the middle of such wealth, were lucky if they could wrestle from the sea just enough pearls to survive.

Lucio padded over the rubble that covered the beach. Through the thin rubber soles of his sandals, made from the automobile tires discarded by the new *gringo* factory, he could feel hundreds of years of history in the generations of broken oyster shells that mixed with the coarse beach sand. Lucio stopped to remove from his sandal a piece of purple shell, rounded and smoothed and made almost translucent by the countless eons of waves that washed into the estuary. He examined it with the intense interest of an expert in such shells, trying to determine its age, wondering if, perhaps, it was part of an oyster that once contained a great pearl. And he considered the man who might have pulled this shell from the sea, and what his life had been like. He wondered if the man might have been related to Lucio in some way. Maybe, he thought, the shell had simply been carried by a hungry gull that dropped the oyster, causing it to smash on the rocks. Often had he seen these birds cheat starvation by such cleverness. Lucio turned the shell over again in his hand, and then he tossed it away.

Carefully he made his way toward the place where he and his neighbors beached the brightly colored fishing boats with their proud, high bows and the short, sturdy masts that could support a small homemade canvas sail. Such boats could easily pull a man over the breakers to the blue waters beyond, where the oysters and the fish played out the drama of their lives.

Lucio's boat lay on the beach above the dark water line of seaweed and foam that marked high tide. Like the other boats, it was painted and plastered, layer upon layer, with the secret formula of preservative known only to the fishermen of La Paz. The secret was something that had been handed down, over the generations, from father to son. Though each of the boats might appear to be the same to the inexperienced eye, each one was different. Each boat had a life, a soul and a personality of its own. Every fisherman took special pride in caring for his boat, which was, at once, his livelihood and his life, his identity and his status in La Paz. And so the fishermen treated them with tenderness and love and respect.

The gleaming surface of Lucio's canoe was painted and decorated with unique and ancient designs that identified this boat as his own. Once it had belonged to his grandfather, Kino, a pearl fisher who was well known and well respected in La Paz. Even nearly a century later, the stories were told of Kino, his wife, Juana, who was Lucio's grandmother, and their first child, Coyotito. They were an important part of the history of the village. And people still told stories of how long ago, the young Kino had once found the "Pearl of the World," the largest, most perfect, most beautiful pearl ever taken from the Gulf waters, a pearl easily worth a hundred thousand *pesos*. They told how Kino's prayers of being a rich man, of having a better life for his family, had been answered. And they told how it had all been taken from him by the evil that came from the city.

There were those old ones still alive who said they remembered, though they were only children then, how Kino, in a final act of defiance against the corruption that had ruined his life, threw his great pearl back into the Gulf in full view of the entire village. These same old ones also told how Kino and Juana's first-born child, Coyotito, had been killed by the evil unleashed from the great pearl. They told how Chance had sent a bullet through the top of the baby's head. These stories endured in the people's hearts, and in their minds. And because they were told over and again, they had become legend in the village, mythical, a central part of the lore for the people who lived there. The story of Kino and Juana's tragedy was taken as a warning to everyone: "Be careful what you wish for. The gods just may give you what you ask." Still there were others who regarded it as a sign of hope.

Lucio knew all of the stories, and he knew the old place at the back of the holy cemetery where worn stone crosses marked the graves of Kino, Juana, and the baby Coyotito, as well as the others who came after, including the recent graves of his own father and mother.

Lucio patted the smooth sides of his boat as one might caress the flank of a horse, or the arm of a loved one. He knew every inch of this boat that had come to him from Kino through his father. Lucio knew even the place at the bottom where once a hole had been broken through. Lucio's father had told his young son the story many times. How the hole had been made by dark forces to prevent Kino and Juana from leaving La Paz with the great pearl to get a fair price for it in Mexico City, more than a thousand miles from La Paz. That was long before Lucio's father had been born. And even though the surface of the canoe had been repaired and restored with years of the secret plaster, Lucio could still trace with his fingers the edge of the break, like the almost faded scar of a wound long healed.

Lucio often thought about these stories, and how his life might have been different if Kino had sold his "Pearl of the World" and kept his fortune of a hundred thousand *pesos*. Then Lucio would have been born into wealth and lived in a real house in the city. It was a pleasant daydream, one that brought a smile to Lucio's face, as he imagined his life as it could have been, but he couldn't afford the luxury of indulging these fantasies for long. Sobering reality told him if he wanted to survive, if he wanted to eat, he had work to do.

Lucio checked to see that all his equipment was ready for the day's fishing -- his old net, repaired many times, his harpoon with a place at the end to tie a line so it wouldn't be lost in the sea or in the back of some large fish, his diving rock and basket, the coils of rope that were his life line. He felt in his belt for his knife. And though some part of Lucio believed that a man was ultimately powerless to change his fate, another part of him knew he had to be prepared for all the possibilities.

A pearl fisher didn't expect pearls. They came by luck. And Lucio knew that Luck was a spoiled child, a fickle lover. The illusive pearls, if there might be any at all, were only faint promise of a man's future. Not every oyster contained a pearl and not every pearl was a good one. A pearl fisher in possession of a pearl then had to sell it to the buyers in the city, and a pearl fisher was at the mercy of these men who were stingy parting with their money.

Sometimes, Lucio knew, in order to change his luck when it was bad, in order to find a pearl when one had eluded him for a long time, he must forget about pearls completely. Sometimes, he knew, he must turn his attention to fishing with a net or a harpoon and turn his back on Luck and on the reluctant pearls. As pleasant as it was to dream of being a rich man, Lucio knew it was better having food to put in his stomach. A fish could be eaten, and some, if the catch was big enough, might be sold. Even just a single fish gave a man life, at least for another day. To Lucio that was reality.

Already the sun was a red blister on the blue sky. Lucio shaded his eyes with his hand and he could see the masts and the sails of some of the other fishers off in the distance. He bent his back against the side of his boat and strained until it grated across the sand and shells, inched along the beach and came alive when it felt the water. Expertly he set the mast and hoisted the sail. The wind that came across the land and carried with it the strange smells from the city filled the orange and blue striped canvas, patched over and again, and pulled the tiny boat and its pilot over the breakers and toward the sun.

The prow cut the calm water like the blade of a sharp knife slices through a man's soft skin. Lucio pressed against the tiller and guided his boat to a place about a half-mile from the shore where the water formed a deep basin. It was not a place he could take oysters because the water was too deep to dive, but it was ideal for fishing. Often the larger fish chased the little ones into the bottom of the pool and trapped them there, feeding until they were sated. The pool was a place of death for the little fish, and it was a place of life as well, for the big fish and for a skillful fisherman who could fill his boat with only a few casts of his net.

Lucio steadied himself and he set the sea anchor that would catch the water and keep the boat from drifting too far. He turned from the late morning sun toward the shore and the light threw his shadow across the top of the water. Lucio reached into the bottom of the boat for his casting net. The circular net was weighted along the edges so it could be thrown. A coiled rope, long enough for casting, connected with another that formed the circumference of the net like a lasso, so that the open net could easily be drawn closed like the top of a sack. It was an ancient and efficient device that had changed little over the centuries, a deadly tool in the hands of a skilled fisherman. Opened, it covered a vast expanse of water. Closed, it became a trap, ensnaring whatever had the misfortune of swimming below the surface in the path of the lethal net.

Lucio felt the boat move under his feet as the gentle swells rose and fell. Off to his right a scatter of silver fish broke the surface of the water. He knew the larger fish were feeding somewhere below him, sending these sweet and tender little ones to the surface. Once more Lucio checked the net, and he looped the end of the casting rope around his wrist. He couldn't afford to lose this net. Then he pulled back his arm and prepared to make his first cast into the center of the school of panicked fish.

His eye caught the movement of a long, dark shadow deeper in the water, and he snapped his arms with the practiced timing of an expert. The weighted net arched out and hung briefly in the air, a perfect circle, before it fell. At the same time a shark's dorsal fin sliced through the water toward the center of its panicked prey. The net landed in the very path of the big fish, causing the shark to alter its course directly toward Lucio's boat.

The shark hit the boat broadside with surprising power and the force of the impact tumbled Lucio into the churning water among the panicked fish. He tried desperately to regain the surface, to lift himself into the boat and out of danger, but the casting rope that enabled him to pull in the fishing net had tightened around Lucio's wrist. He fumbled with the wet rope, but the slipknot wouldn't yield. The net was caught around the shark's nose, snagged in the teeth of its gaping mouth. The startled, powerful fish turned and dragged Lucio deeper under the water, trailing him like the tail attached to the end of a child's kite.

Normally Lucio could hold his breath for more than three minutes while he searched for pearls, but he had managed only a short breath before the shark pulled him down and the waters closed around him. Frantically he struggled to reach the knife in his belt to cut himself free. The pain was intense as the power of the startled fish almost pulled Lucio's arm from its socket, and the taut rope tightened even more around his wrist, stopping the flow of blood to his hand.

The shark picked up speed, taking Lucio lower and lower to where the filtered light formed eerie shadows on the sand. The pressure pressed in on Lucio's ears and made his lungs feel as if they would explode. Lucio slashed desperately with his knife, but another sudden tug from the shark jerked out his arm just as the sharp blade sliced through rope and skin. Lucio's heart was pounding and the constricted flow of his blood, suddenly released when the rope was severed, pumped like a dark cloud into the water. The effect on the shark was immediate. It seemed to hesitate for just a second, scenting the water, and then made a wide turn, to find this new source of food.

The shark came up from below, directly at Lucio, with its craggy mouth opened wide. Its dark, dead eyes were visible through the net that was still draped over the shark's face and was caught in the triangular teeth. Lucio jabbed at one eye with his knife and pulled on the fishing net with his other hand, trying to tighten it around the shark's jaws, or change its direction. Blood from his wound washed into the shark's mouth, jolting it like an electric shock or the first sharp taste of alcohol. The shark jerked to the left as Lucio swam down and to the right, heading for the bottom. Trailing blood, Lucio scrambled into a small grotto between two large rocks, just ahead of the lunging shark. Lucio's head ached. His chest felt compressed, as under a huge weight, and his lungs were ready to burst. He was dizzy from the lack of oxygen and the loss of blood. He could feel his vision fading and his mind clouding. He knew he had only a few more seconds before he would drown.

With every ounce of strength that remained, Lucio prayed frantically to the Virgin Mary, to his dead parents, to Kino, Juana and to all his dead relatives. And then a little miracle happened in the form of a bright orange fish that swam directly into the path of the frenzied shark. Lucio watched as the frustrated predator took the fish with a snap of its huge jaws, shaking it viciously and breaking it in two. Then, as suddenly as it had come, the shark swam away and disappeared into the shadows.

Lucio whispered a quick prayer of thanks to God the Father and the other ancient gods of his ancestors. Looking down, he saw the reflection of something shiny on the sandy bottom between the rocks where he was hidden. He grabbed for it and closed the hand of his injured arm around the object. His legs kicked off the sandy bottom like a taut spring, and Lucio swam frantically for the surface, his lungs screaming for air.

When his head broke through the water he saw that his boat was less than twenty yards away. In seconds he had pulled himself over the side and he was safe. With the blood still pumping from the gash in his arm, Lucio wrapped it with a piece of fishing line he found on the bottom of the boat, tying off the knot with his teeth. He watched as the flow of blood eventually slowed and almost stopped.

It was then that Lucio saw the fist of his injured arm was still tightly closed. Slowly and painfully he had to pry open his fingers with his other hand. Lucio stared in disbelief and his mouth dropped open with the surprise of what he saw. In the bloody palm of his hand he held a large and beautiful pearl, one such as Lucio had never seen before. This was the pearl of his dreams.

A small stream of Lucio's blood trickled down his arm, and it mixed with the essence of the pearl, so that the two, Lucio and the pearl, became one, before his eyes closed and he passed out.

Chapter Two

Lucio awakened on the sleeping cot inside his house. His thoughts were foggy and his body ached. He couldn't remember how he had made it back to shore, or if he even had the strength to pull his boat onto the beach. All he could remember was the beautiful pearl.

"The pearl!" Lucio said out loud and the sound of his words startled him. There was panic in his voice and in his heart, for there was no sign of the great pearl anywhere. It was gone. And then a sad thought came into Lucio's head, that it must have all been a wonderfully terrible dream induced by the lack of oxygen under the water. Perhaps, he thought, he was asleep the entire time and that he had never even been out on his boat. Perhaps it had *all* been an illusion. But when Lucio tried to move, the stiffness in his arm and the pain that he felt, told him that some of it, at least, hadn't been a dream. The wound, he saw, was real, and it was cleaned and freshly bandaged. Even if there hadn't been a pearl, he took some consolation that at least he was alive.

Then Lucio heard a rustling sound that came through the window from outside his house, and suddenly he was afraid again. He grabbed the long knife, a machete that had once belonged to his father. With some difficulty he pulled himself up from his cot and he rushed to the door. By the length and the angle of the shadows he knew that it was late in the afternoon. Most of the day had slipped away from him, just as his pearl had slipped through his fingers.

His left hand tightened on the handle of the knife and he faced the familiar figure of Corina. "You!" he said. She was holding vegetables she had just picked from the little plot that Lucio kept as a garden.

"You are awake at last. I thought you might sleep until the Fiesta of Santa Rosalia," Corina said gently and she smiled before she lowered her eyes. Although she knew Lucio from when they were children, she was still very shy and modest when she spoke to him. "I was just preparing some supper for you."

His head was full of questions. "How did I get here from the boat?" Lucio asked, looking at her face for any sign of the pearl.

"My father and Clementé, and some of the other men. They found you on the beach. You were bleeding and unconscious. They brought you here and my father told me to look after you until he returned. I cleaned and bandaged your wound. There is a deep cut on your arm."

"Did they-" he hesitated. "Was there anything? Anything else?" He found it hard to finish his thought.

She lowered her voice to a whisper. "I found your pearl, Lucio," she said. "It was clenched so tightly in your hand I had to pull it away from you. You don't have to worry. No one else knows. No one else saw it."

He was relieved. He was elated and his heart began to pound in his chest. And then he looked deeply into Corina's eyes.

"I hid it from the others," she said, answering the question that he hadn't asked. "I didn't tell them, not even my father. Your pearl is safe. I buried it here in your garden." She pointed to a place where the earth was dark between the stringy stalks of beans.

Lucio rushed past her and he began to dig in the soft earth with his good hand and then with his machete, until he found the piece of dirty leather in which she had wrapped the pearl. He held it in his hand. With his awkward, hurting fingers he unwrapped the pearl and dropped it into his palm. The beauty of the pearl reflected the light of the late afternoon sun, and the brightness almost blinded Lucio.

"I am a rich man," he whispered excitedly to Corina. "Richer beyond anything I ever dreamed." He was unable to take his eyes from the beauty of the pearl, as his mind flooded with so many thoughts. "This pearl is my future. It is the answer to all of my prayers." His head was spinning. "With some of the money I get from the sale of this pearl, I will go to the old priest and pay to have him say so many masses for my dead parents, that I will move their souls from Purgatory into Heaven. And the souls of many others. No longer will I have to worry about having enough food to eat. Or clothes. My future is assured, Corina, as it has never been." He was out of breath from talking so many words at one time, more words than Corina had heard him say to her in all the time she knew him.

And although Corina was excited by Lucio's excitement, and elated by his unexpected good fortune, she was disappointed too, in his words. She had always loved Lucio, ever since she could remember. Always she had assumed that they would be married when the day came. It was something he had promised her when they were still children. Yet now there was no indication in his plans that this would be so. And that disappointment showed on her face.

Lucio saw the shadow of darkness move across her face. "Why do you look so sad, Corina? Aren't you happy for me?"

"Of course I am happy, Lucio," she said, and she paused as she searched for the right words. "I love you as you are. I have, always. I don't want this fortune to turn your head. To make a different man of you, Lucio." But already she thought she could sense a change in him. "You said this pearl is *your* future. Always I thought *I* was part of your future too. What future do you see for me in your pearl? What do you see for *us*?"

Lucio stared into the beauty of the pearl, and then he looked into her sad, dark eyes. "We *will* be married, Corina" he said quickly. He closed his hand over the pearl and cut off the light. "I said that we would. And when I have the money, I will go to the priest in the city and arrange for the church. I promise."

Then Lucio's mind turned to other promises, the ones he had made to God, his pledge to donate one tenth of the value of the pearl to the church, to give money to the poor. Of course, he told himself, he would do what he had said. But a part of him wondered if God would really hold him so strictly to such promises made in haste. And Lucio's mind reeled with other prospects he had never before considered possible, the things he could buy now, the life he could live. Lucio threw his head back and he howled at the top of his voice like a wild animal freed from a trap. "I am a rich man!" he called.

The shout startled Corina, and it brought his neighbors tumbling out of their houses to discover the disturbance. They crowded into the yard around Lucio and Corina.

Over his head Lucio held the great pearl in the fingers of his bandaged hand. He turned slowly so all his neighbors could see the extent of his good fortune. Women hugged their children and covered their eyes in disbelief. The mouths of the other pearl fishers gaped wide. There were gasps at the size and the beauty of Lucio's pearl.

"I am a rich man," he said. "When I go to the pearl buyers in the city I will claim my great fortune. I am a rich man!"

Chapter Three

Word of Lucio's pearl seemed to spread on the warm Gulf breeze that blew through the houses of the little village. It was the topic of conversation in every house. Late in the afternoon his neighbors crowded around to marvel at Lucio's good fortune, and to envy him as well. In the crowd surrounding him there were those who were genuinely happy for Lucio, but there were also those who smiled in Lucio's face and secretly wished that the pearl belonged to them. In some of the people who filled his house that wish brought another wish, that Lucio didn't exist so they could own his pearl. Their fingers itched to have his pearl, and their secret desires set into motion many plans to get it.

Word of the pearl spread beyond the boundary that separated the poor fishermen from those who lived in the crowded city of La Paz. Though no one there knew exactly who Lucio was, they too were glad for his unanticipated fortune. For the people of the city knew that a poor Indian with money was an easy mark. And at once, as soon as they heard the news, there were those who began hatching schemes to separate Lucio from his newly found wealth.

Word of the pearl reached the old priest who was kneeling at the altar of the church, offering prayers to the Holy Virgin for the souls of those who had the money to pay him for such spiritual favors. The news made him smile, and the thoughts of what he could do with some of the money from the pearl made him lose count on the beads of his rosary. The priest knew that his very existence and that of his church depended on these poor, simple and ignorant Indians and their contributions. He well knew these people who were so full of fears and superstitions, as he knew the power of religion that he exerted over them, wielding it and the threat of eternal damnation as a sword, striking fear in the minds and hearts of the people who made up his parish.

Five hundred years before, when Cortez and his *conquistadors* subjugated Lucio's people, it was only in part because of the fine Toledo steel that they carried in their Spanish blades. The strangers, welcomed as gods, unleashed another more subtle and more powerful weapon on the Indians, one that literally brought them to their knees. It was not the black powder in their guns, but the black robed friars who carried with them a message from the Holy Father in Rome. These warrior-priests spread the word among the native people of the New World with a fiery zeal. The fire burned through the Indians, scorching back their old heathen gods and making room for the marvelous three-in-one God of Christianity, Father, Son and Holy Ghost. The symbol of this new religion was the cross of gold. The Spaniards brought the cross and they took the gold. The Indians were quick to embrace with all of their hearts the faith of saints and miracles. But the religion of the white conquerors was used not just to bring their heathen souls salvation in Heaven, but as the means of controlling their hearts and minds, and their bodies here on earth. The Christian message, more powerful than sudden death by gun or sword, was clear: total obedience -- to God, to King, to Church and to Master -- or eternal damnation.

The old priest was shrewd. He understood that his power was greater even than the power of a doctor. For a doctor who refuses to treat a sick man can only hasten that man's death and shorten his suffering in this world. But a priest who ministers to a man's spiritual needs controls that man's life for eternity. Such power was to be respected and to be feared. The old priest also knew that an Indian with money would be only too eager to spend some of it and rescue the souls of dead relatives from the fires of Purgatory and send them ever closer to the haven of Heaven. An Indian with money would be happy to pay in advance, as an insurance policy, for enough prayers and blessings and masses to speed his own soul along on its journey into Paradise after death. All of this the priest knew while he counted another Hail Mary on his beads. And the priest was determined to visit Lucio at his first opportunity.

Word of Lucio's pearl blew into the offices of the pearl buyers. In La Paz they were the modern alchemists, able to turn pearls into gold and gold into food. They knew that a pearl, for all of its beauty, is valueless to a man with hunger in his stomach, and that a pearl cannot protect a man and his family from the elements. The buyers knew that this fortunate fisher would have to come to them with his treasure if he wanted to eat, if he wanted new clothes, if he wanted a better life. Already there were those plotting strategies to get this great pearl at the lowest price.

Word of the pearl burned into the minds of others in La Paz, some who were strangers and some who were Lucio's neighbors, and it made them envious. They smiled on his good fortune in the day, but secretly in the darkness, when their thoughts ran free, shielded by the night, they dared to dream their plans. And they would stop at nothing to get their hands on Lucio's pearl.

Lucio wasn't totally ignorant of such things. From the sermons made in the church by the old priest, he was aware of the evil that might live in the heart of even the best person, and he knew the story of Kino. Then an interesting thought came to him. Perhaps this was the very pearl lost by his grandfather. Maybe, he considered, God had brought him the same pearl to make amends for the terrible injustice suffered by Kino. And his thoughts made Lucio determined and wise, but it also made him afraid. Because he was afraid, he knew he had to take great care to protect what was his. He was determined to hold on to his dreams, and not throw them back into the sea as Kino had done.

In the evening, when he was alone, Lucio lit a piece of consecrated candle and took his pearl. It felt warm and alive in his hand. He turned it between his thumb and his index finger, as one might examine a chicken's egg, for the pearl was that large. Its color and its curve were perfect. For a long time Lucio stared into its lovely surface and the reflected light of the flickering candle hypnotized him, so that he wasn't aware that his face was smiling.

Later he wrapped the pearl in a clean piece of soft leather, and he searched for a safe place to hide it until he could sell it in the city, as he had said he would. When all that was done Lucio fell asleep.

He was sitting at an enormous wooden table, elaborately decorated with flowers and piled high with the finest foods. The table was not in his house, but in the large banquet hall of one of the grandest hotels in La Paz, recently built to cater to the ever-growing number of vacationing *gringos*. It was a place Lucio had once seen when he had delivered a catch of fresh fish to feed the *Americano* tourists and the wealthy business men who used the banquet hall to close their deals for more land and power. Brightly lit and festooned with colorful streamers, the hall vibrated with laughter of unseen people, the thrum and the rhythm of many Mexican guitars and the pulsating warmth of gleaming trumpets. Lucio's head swam with the extravagance of it all -- the half finished bottles of wine, the uneaten food that could easily have fed all the people of his village at least one substantial meal.

Beside him sat Corina, dressed in a beautiful gown that was trimmed with fine lace. Her young face was radiant and flushed pink with wine and with the excitement of the day's events. It was their wedding *fiesta*.

Lucio raised his crystal glass in a toast to celebrate their happiness. Then, as the music played, a dark shadow passed over the scene and everything changed. A chill ran through Lucio as he turned to look at his beautiful young wife. But Corina was gone. In her place was the form of a bloated old woman, a hag, whose smile was a toothless grin that mocked him and made Lucio's blood run cold. He tipped his glass to drink the rich red wine, but the taste was bitter, the sour grapes of wrath. The food was dry and tasteless in his mouth, and everything turned to ashes. The faces of his friends became the frightening stares of strangers closing in on him. Their greedy hands pulled at him, tearing his fine new wedding suit to rags.

In the midst of this terror Lucio called out and he swung his arms in combat. Then he was fully awake. It had been a dream, a nightmare.

The night air felt cool against the perspiration on Lucio's damp body. He lay in the darkness trying to control his rapid breathing and to slow the pounding of his racing heart. He listened to the noises in the night, the distant waves breaking on the rubbly beach, and the sound of tiny tree frogs that sounded almost like the songs of birds. When Lucio was calm and certain that he was in no danger, his eyes fluttered and he was ready to turn over on his cot and try to sleep again, grateful that it had all been just a horrible nightmare.

Then, from somewhere in the darkness of his room, the sound of some alien thing came to his ears and Lucio was alert and afraid all over again. He strained to listen for the thing that didn't belong, the tiny exhalation of someone breathing in the darkness in his home, the pulse of someone else's heart beating. He was sure that the sound had come from close by and the thought made the hairs on the back of Lucio's head stand on end.

Lucio was about to move, about to reach slowly for the machete that he kept near his cot. But before he finished the thought, a pair of strong hands pinned Lucio's arms like the jaws of an iron vice and lifted him roughly from the cot. At the same time he felt a coarse burlap sack thrown over his head, closing off what little sight he had and almost stopping his breath. Muffled by the hood, Lucio could hear the crash of things breaking as the intruders began a frantic search for where the pearl was hidden, turning the contents of his house upside down. There were at least two of them, Lucio knew, the one who was holding on to him and the other who was searching. Perhaps there were more.

When the initial panic cleared from his brain and his fear began to wane, Lucio grew angry with these invaders who showed him no respect and violated his home. And his anger formulated into a plan. Carefully he moved his foot, feeling for the machete that he knew was by the bed. When he touched it with his toe he was encouraged. Now if only he could get to it, he could fight.

Then Lucio felt the cold steel of a knife blade pressed against his throat, and he heard the harsh voice of a man. "The pearl, *amigo*," the voice said icily. "If you want to continue to live, tell us where you have hidden the pearl."

With the sound of the words all fear was gone from Lucio, for deep inside he felt an inner strength that brought with it courage. Of course he wanted to live, but he would not have what was his taken from him, even if it meant he had to die. Lucio was willing and ready to die for his pearl. Dying like a man was preferred to living like a coward. It was a matter of pride, and pride was so important to people who had so little else to lose.

"You will not kill me," Lucio replied with his newly found strength. He made his words sound calm and assured. "If you kill me, you will *never* find the pearl."

"Perhaps." The whispered word was loud in Lucio's head, as his captor's lips were so close they brushed the canvass sack.

Lucio's arrogant response had caused the other man to slide the knife lightly across Lucio's neck, from his left ear to his Adam's apple. The blade was so sharp that even this light pressure was enough to bring the blood from under his skin. There was no pain, but Lucio felt the warm, sticky trickle flow down his neck and spread on his shirt. "If you will die now still remains to be seen, *amigo*," the man said.

There was something familiar in the sound of the voice, and Lucio strained to identify who it might be. He drew a deep breath, and at the same time he felt the man's grip on his arms slacken, just for a second. And Lucio was in motion. He twisted his arms free and pulled at the hood on his head in one quick motion, but it was stuck and his vision was still obscured. Instinctively, Lucio ducked to the right, avoiding the thrust of the knife, and he grabbed for the horn handle of the machete by his feet.

His sudden, unexpected escape surprised his captors long enough for Lucio to counter, to whirl and lunge at the one with the knife. Lucio slashed him with his heavy machete and felt his blade cut through cloth. He heard the man moan and the rush of his startled breath. Then Lucio struck wildly, blindly at the other and his heavy knife hit home. He pulled the hood from his head and in the darkness he saw only the broad back of one man retreating through the open doorway. He raised his machete and took a step in pursuit, but the man was gone. Too late Lucio thought of the other man. But when he did, the intruder had broken through the screen and he too was already swallowed by the night.

Lucio peered hard into the darkness, but all he could see was the wave of the shadows in the night breeze. His hand rested on the window frame and his fingers felt sticky. He looked and saw the traces of blood on the wooden sill and on his hand. The knowledge that he had wounded both of them gave Lucio some satisfaction. A man with a knife cut would be easier to find in the daylight, he thought.

Then Lucio inspected his own wound and the damage that was done to his house. Everything was overturned and scattered across the floor. His cot was broken and the stuffing pulled out of his mattress. The shelves on the wall had been cleared with little concern for the treasures they contained -- his mother's favorite plate, a plaster statue of the Virgin, the faded sepia portrait of his parents, now with the glass broken in the wooden frame. They were all mingled together on the floor in an unrepairable confusion of glass shards and broken pottery. It made Lucio sad and angry. But the men hadn't found his pearl, and that made Lucio glad.

He closed and secured the wooden door by bracing it shut with the back of a chair. He looked out carefully through the opened window, making sure that he wasn't being watched from outside. Then he pulled the old curtain across the broken screen and shut out the night. Lucio went to the tumble of cans that had been thrown in the corner and he picked through them until he found the one that he wanted, a tin half full of cooking lard. He dug his still bloody hand into the hardened fat, feeling for the prize with the tips of his fingers. Finding it, he pulled it out and carefully unwrapped and uncovered his precious pearl. He had won this battle.

But even in his little victory Lucio felt the twinges of despair. He knew that the men would be watching him and that they would not give up until they had what they came for. He had to find a place of safety for his pearl. And then a thought came to him.

Chapter Four

Lucio worked quickly in the darkness. Only after he had wrapped his pearl in a clean piece of leather and placed it in a secret pocket under his shirt did he strike a wooden match on the tabletop. The flare of the match threw the room into harsh light and he was startled by the shadows that jumped out at him like ghosts. When he was reassured that there was nothing to fear, he held the sputtering match to the wick of an old oil lantern and he turned the flame down until it was only a pale glow. Instantly the shadowy ghosts in the room receded back into the walls.

Lucio grabbed the handle of his machete, and he let the long knife hang down at his side, ready to be raised in an instant if he needed to defend himself. Carefully and quietly he opened the door and he listened to the sounds of the night for any signs that might indicate the presence of some unusual thing. But the tree frogs had once again picked up the rhythm of their songs and the hum of insects and the chirrup of crickets played the melody. When Lucio was convinced that it was safe, he slipped into the cover of the brush. If anyone was watching the house, he thought, they would be fooled by the lantern light, and they would think that he was still inside. He hoped the light might keep them at bay, at least until he found a safe hiding place for his pearl.

In the darkness mosquitoes flew about his face, drawn by the sweet scent of his blood. He could feel their tiny bites on his face and neck, but Lucio paid them no attention. His eyes were intent for any movement and his ears were alert for any sound that wasn't part of the night. By the position of the stars Lucio knew that it was well past midnight.

Silently he slipped through the shadows and then broke into a run. Lucio stumbled, and when he looked he saw that it was the body of a man lying in the brush. Holding his machete in defense, Lucio prodded the body with his hand and when there was no response, he carefully rolled the man over. What he saw made him very sad. It was Clementé, a friend of his father's, a man Lucio knew from when he was a child and he was there, dead in the road with a large knife wound across his throat. This confused Lucio. Had poor Clementé been so unlucky to come upon Lucio's fleeing attackers in the darkness, only to have his throat cut? And then another possibility occurred to Lucio that turned his sadness and his confusion into anger. Could it have been Clementé who came into Lucio's house not an hour ago? Lucio thought he had recognized the man's voice. Lucio might have understood if it had been a stranger, but why would a neighbor, a friend, someone Lucio had known his entire life, try to steal the pearl and try to kill him? Seeing Clementé with his lifeblood seeping into the dark earth Lucio wondered who the other man could have been. He shook his head in despair and to clear the pain that he felt.

He pushed Clementé's body deeper into the brush, but he knew that it would be discovered, cold and stiff, in the morning by the men going to their boats. And when they saw who it was, those who found Clementé would wonder what had happened to cause his violent death. There would be many questions asked. Lucio too would demand answers, in the morning. But for now his only concern was to hide his pearl.

He struck out into the brush, leaving a visible trail away from his village. He hoped that any other pursuers would think he was heading under cover of the night to Loreto in the north. For almost an hour he went, changing his direction often, weaving back and forth, crossing over his trail to make it difficult, but not impossible for those who might try to follow him. For he wanted any pursuers to think he was trying to cover his tracks, but he wanted them to follow. Always Lucio headed north, and always he left a little sign here, a careless footprint there, a broken branch, a little mark in the trail for any tracker to find.

When Lucio was satisfied with his work, he spent the next hour walking a wide half circle toward the west. These tracks he covered carefully, leaving no trace of his deception. In the darkness, before dawn, Lucio secretly returned to his village from the south.

Everything was silent and empty, for most of the people were still asleep. The only stirring came from the early morning roosters preparing to signal the approaching sunrise. He listened to the rustle of pigs searching in the brush to uncover some forgotten thing to eat, and the occasional yelping of dogs mating in the darkness. All these sounds carried over the night to him.

Lucio stopped when he came to the familiar house of Corina and her parents. He knew that they would be asleep. He listened from the shadows and waited. As close as he was to this family, it would be improper for Lucio to visit their daughter, or even enter their home, without the permission of Ernesto and Heléna. He would never enter the house of *any* man without an invitation. That was the unwritten law. In a place where a man owned little, his house was his only sanctuary, never to be violated. But these were not ordinary circumstances, and right or wrong, Lucio had decided that the only chance he had to hold on to his pearl was Corina.

With the stealth and the agility of a cat, he climbed up to the window where he knew Corina slept. His ragged fingers scratched on the screening.

In a moment there was a frightened reply. "Who is there?" he heard her startled, sleepy voice call from inside, and then he saw Corina's surprised face by the window. "Lucio," she said, confused by his appearance, "why are you here? It is still very dark." She clutched her sleeping gown around her modestly. Then she saw the wound on his neck and the terrible look in his eyes. "You are hurt. What has happened to you, Lucio?"

"The pearl," he said. "They came to take away my pearl in the night. Two of them. But I fought them. I wounded a man and–" He hesitated. "I killed another. In the brush near my house is the body of Clementé."

"Clementé?" she asked in disbelief. "You are sure?"

"As sure as I know that I still have my pearl. He was one of them."

"And the other?"

"I don't know," he said. "But I will find him in the daylight. His wound will give him away." Lucio looked around at the darkness. "I must come inside, Corina. I am afraid someone will see me here."

Corina hesitated. She turned away and listened for the sleeping sounds that came from the other room. Then carefully and quietly she pulled open the screen. "Oh, Lucio," she said when she saw the extent of his wounds. "Look what this pearl has already done to you."

She took one of the candles that burned in front of the statue of the Holy Virgin, and she found a clean piece of cloth. She moistened it with some Holy Water blessed by the priest and kept in her room as a safeguard against the demons that ran about so freely in the night. Gently she cleaned the dried blood from Lucio's neck. The sting and pressure made him wince.

"My father was right," she said. "I heard him speaking this evening with the other men from the village. They all agreed that it would only bring you misery, just as it did for Kino. And already it has happened. I think this pearl too is cursed, Lucio. It frightens me."

"If you are afraid, Corina, perhaps I should not be here to ask you for your help." He took the pearl from its secret place under his shirt and he held it in his hand so that she could see its beauty.

The sparkle of the pearl almost made her dizzy. But when Corina saw it again the tension in her relaxed. "You may ask anything of me, Lucio. You know I will always help you."

He handed the pearl over to her. "Hide it then. In the safest place where no one will think to look," he said. "If they come again for the pearl they will come after me. But I will be ready for them next time. Tell no one that you have it. Not even your father or your mother." He touched her on the cheek. "This pearl is our chance to be married."

"The Father in the church tells many stories of how the Devil comes with greed to possess a man's soul. And I am afraid for you." She continued, "But I will do as you say, Lucio."

"Don't worry," he reassured her, "I will be all right. When it is safe I will return for the pearl. After I have sold it we will be married," he said, and his words were a promise that made her happy, as she watched him climb through the window and back into the night.

Corina closed her hand around the pearl, cutting off the light. Then she thought about the safest place to hide their pearl.

Chapter Five

To draw any danger away from Corina and her parents, Lucio took an indirect path back to his house, but one not nearly as complex. Darkness was fighting off the dawn, so when Lucio saw the glow ahead of him he knew it wasn't the sun. He gripped the handle of his machete tightly and his suspicion urged him to run as fast as he could. But before he had cleared the brush he saw the flames leaping into the sky and licking at the low night clouds. It was his house that was burning.

From his place of concealment in the brush, Lucio could see many of his neighbors running about. Some were in their yards watching the growing flames with concern for the safety of their own homes. Others rushed toward the flames to be of some assistance. All was chaos. Sleeping children, shaken from their dreams by the shouts of the adults, moaned with fear. Women cried into their shawls, for they knew that no one could survive such a quick and intense fire. Certain that the handsome, young Lucio was dead, they sent up their prayers for his soul.

Only yesterday, some said, Lucio was a rich man, with all his dreams about to be fulfilled, with a life of ease ahead of him, guaranteed by his pearl. And everyone was quick to wish that they might change places with him. But now his life was ended. The great pearl had not been able to save him. And all were glad that it was not they who had come to such a terrible death in the fire. It was a shame, they agreed, the irony of it, the tricks often played on man by God, who gave with one hand and took with the other.

Amid the shouts and confusion, neighbors rushed to wet down their own houses to keep them from igniting by the flying sparks and being consumed. Then, only after ensuring the safety of their own homes, did they concern themselves with Lucio's and join those who poured water on the flames. But it was too late and everyone knew it. And from his hiding place Lucio knew it as well. Everything he owned had been destroyed, everything but his boat that was tied securely on the beach. And his pearl.

Those who started the fire knew that Lucio hadn't been there inside the house and they would still come looking for him. Lucio watched the features of his neighbors as the dying light from the burning house played across their faces. He wondered which one of them might have come into his house in the night with Clementé. He also wondered if some of the very men now trying to put out the blaze might also be the ones who had started it.

Lucio sank back into the darkness away from the hot glow of the fire. He hoped that he would have enough time in the confusion to steal away from La Paz before the sun was up, before his neighbors sifted through the ashes and discovered that he was not dead. Lucio began to tremble, but not from the cold of the early morning air. He was afraid again, afraid for himself and afraid for Corina. If he had been followed, giving the pearl to Corina only put her and her parents in great danger. But even if he had not been seen, those who wanted his pearl would think of Corina too, and they would go into her house, just as they had come into his. Perhaps even now they were there, he thought. And Lucio was angry with himself for being so stupid and so selfish, for not having thought of Corina's safety first.

Lucio ducked into the brush, and he started back the way he had come. His senses were dulled. His racing mind was preoccupied as he hurried along the path, keeping himself in the decreasing shadows. He wasn't thinking of his own safety now, but of Corina, and of course, his pearl.

He heard the sound of the attack at the same time that he felt the crack on the back of his head. The blow made his head explode with stars, bright constellations, that some part inside of him admired even as he dropped to his knees. His machete slipped from his hand. He wanted to fight back, but his arms and legs felt like lead, and he moved as a man under water, in slow motion, as in his nightmares where he is attacked and unable to run from his pursuers. All of these thoughts went through Lucio's mind in a flash.

In his semi-consciousness he could feel angry hands tear through his clothing, pulling at his shirt and his pants. He was helpless and immobilized, as a man lying in a coma who hears the words of his relatives crying for his condition, but unable to respond. He heard the ripping sound of material and then in his side he felt a sharp kick that sent Lucio all the way into darkness.

Lucio lay on the hard-caked ground for some time. When he finally awakened it was almost daylight. The sun, hiding just below the eastern horizon, made a pink glow in the clouds that hung low over the Gulf. Lucio shook his head to clear the pain and to collect his thoughts. His right side ached. He rubbed the place on his head where it was swollen, and when he pulled his hand away it was covered red with his blood and with ants. Then from the corner of his eye Lucio saw the long lines of insects streaming out of the brush and across his body. Fire ants they were called, because of the painful burning sting they inflicted on their prey. Lucio had seen the carcass of a dead goat stripped clean to the bones by an army of these ever-hungry scavengers. Now, through some innate sense, the smell of his blood, or perhaps some unheard language communicated by advance scouts to the whole community, the colony of ants had been stirred into action, drawn from their nest deep under the ground to consume him.

Lucio felt the numbing, burning pinch of hundreds of tiny jaws as they feasted on his body and his blood. He got to his feet with some difficulty. He pulled at the ants and slapped at his torn shirt and his pants. He crushed those, still clinging to him, still biting him in a final act of stubborn defiance before their own deaths. When he had shaken most of the ants from him, he searched the brush until he found his machete. Then Lucio stumbled directly on toward Corina's house. He hoped that he wasn't too late.

When Lucio approached the house he saw Heléna standing dazed and confused in the open doorway. Her eyes grew wide with fright when she recognized Lucio coming closer. She dropped down on her knees and prayed, making the Sign of the Cross and she kissing her fingers. It was as though she was seeing a ghost.

"Heléna," he said as he took in the condition of her house at a glance. Heléna was standing in the middle of the floor, surrounded by the debris of what had once been her entire life.

His voice seemed to shake her out of a trance. "Lucio, you are alive!" She was shivering with fear, but she grew calmer when she realized that he was real and not a spirit. She saw his injuries. "You are badly hurt."

"I am well enough. But what has happened here?" he asked. "Who has done this? Where is Corina?" His questions came in a steady stream as he tried to understand all that had taken place.

Heléna was in tears. "I don't know. It is all a confusion in my mind. In the night I heard the shouts of fire and I ran out to see what was happening. I heard the people in the village crying. Some said that you were dead. And when I returned to tell Corina the terrible news, she was gone. The house was as you see it now." She picked up the remains of a clay pot. "Everything is broken. Hardly anything remains." She wiped her tears. "And why?" she asked looking into his eyes for the answer. "Why would someone do this to us? We had so little. And now we have nothing."

"It is the pearl," Lucio said. "They have come again for my pearl."

"Your pearl?" Heléna didn't understand. "What does your pearl have to do with this?"

"Last night I was attacked. Clementé and another came into my house and tried to steal my pearl. Now Clementé is dead and the other carries a wound from my knife. When you were asleep I came here in the cover of darkness and I gave the pearl to Corina to hide for me. It was a mistake that I regret. Then my house was burned. On my way here to recover the pearl and take the danger from you and Corina I was attacked a second time. Heléna, I am sorry for the trouble I have brought to you and your husband. And to Corina. Perhaps it would have been better if they had taken the pearl." Then a thought came to him. "Where is Ernesto?"

"I don't know," she said. "He went out last night to check his boat and he never returned. When I awoke this morning he was not in our bed. I thought he might have gone to help with the fire, but I didn't see him. He has disappeared along with Corina." After she said this there was great fear in her voice. "Lucio, this pearl has brought evil to all of us." Heléna wrung her hands.

"Yes, the pearl," he said. "What has happened to my pearl?"

"This pearl is evil, Lucio. It would be a blessing if it were taken. If it were gone forever. If it was never found."

Lucio turned from her. "I must go now to find Corina and Ernesto," he said. "And then we will see about the pearl."

Lucio knew where to begin his search and he ran down to the beach toward Ernesto's boat. Often Ernesto spent long hours there repairing his nets and caring for the equipment upon which his life and the lives of Heléna and Corina depended. It was the one thing the old fisherman loved most, after his family. It had been Ernesto even more than his own father who had taught Lucio that a boat was not just wood and paint, that it was alive and that it possessed a spirit, linked to the spirits of those dead who had come before them. Many times in the evenings, long after the other fishermen had left for their houses, or in the early mornings, before the others were even awake, Lucio had seen Ernesto praying to the spirit of his boat. Now Lucio found his old friend asleep in the bottom of the boat among the broken shards of an empty bottle of tequila that lay smashed beside him.

"Ernesto," he called, shaking him from his drunken sleep.

"Leave me," the man protested. "Leave me." Ernesto pushed Lucio's hand away. "Let me sleep. Leave me to my misery."

Lucio grabbed him by the shoulders and shook him. The man cried out in pain and pulled back.

"Wake up, Ernesto. It is Lucio. You are asleep. You are drunk. Where is Corina? Was she with you? Have you seen her?" His questions came too quickly and the old fisherman was too drunk and too confused to answer.

Slowly Ernesto came around. He shook his head to clear his thoughts. "Ah, Lucio," he said, "it is you." He felt the pain of too much tequila in his brain. His words were slow and slurred. "I am sorry, Lucio. You know that I love you like my own son. And I am so very sorry." He tried to get up, but he was unsteady and unable to do so. The intense pain in his shoulder made him wince. When it passed Ernesto took a deep breath.

"You are hurt, my friend. What has happened to your arm?" Lucio tried to help him up. He took Ernesto's arm and saw a long cut crusted with dried blood. It started at his right shoulder and ended on the muscle of his old, strong arm. "Ernesto, what has happened to you? You have been badly hurt."

Ernesto put him off with a wave of his hands and then he managed to get to his feet with some difficulty. He rubbed the place on his shoulder and his arm. "It is no matter," he said. "Last night I stumbled in the darkness and I was cut on the broken glass. Heléna is right. I drink too much, Lucio. And now, sleeping on the bottom of this boat has made a foolish old man stiff and sore." He saw the wounds on Lucio and he winced.

"This is nothing," Lucio said, reading the expression on the old man's face.

When Ernesto spoke again his voice was subdued. "What is this you said about Corina?" he asked.

"She was not at home. I have just come from there." Lucio told him the events of the night, the two attacks, the death of Clementé, his first visit to Corina and the fire. But it was as though Ernesto wasn't really listening.

"You gave your pearl to my daughter?" he said absently and there was fear in his voice. "Then you have put her in great danger, Lucio. I am afraid your pearl will be the undoing of us all." He shook his head again to clear his thoughts. "Such a pearl may cause even a good man as Clementé to do things he would be sorry for afterwards. It has such blinding power it may make a man ashamed of things he's done–" He squeezed Lucio's hand like a child holding on to a parent for protection.

Lucio didn't understand Ernesto's words, but he attributed them to the tequila and the damp night sleeping in his boat. He didn't have any time to waste. There were other considerations on his mind. "Take care of yourself, Ernesto. Now I must go and find Corina," Lucio said.

"I will come with you," Ernesto said, trying to become himself again.

"No. I can go more quickly alone. You go back to your house and help Heléna, for they were there already to look for the pearl. Have her tend to your wound."

"Wait for me!" he said, but Ernesto gave up his protest when he was unable to steady himself. "Yes," he said, "you are right. Go and find Corina. Protect her, Lucio. I know those who want your pearl will stop at nothing to get it." He looked at Lucio and there were tears again in his drunken old eyes. He said again, "I'm so very sorry for you, my son. For all of us. And for Clementé, who was my friend."

Lucio turned from him and he ran back along the beach toward the village. Ernesto's words were in his head. His injury was serious, but it was clean and deep, clear to the muscle, more like a knife wound than a cut from glass. And then a thought came into his head, but he couldn't face the possibilities and he dismissed his foolishness from his mind. Lucio broke through the line of brush as these questions played in his head.

And then he saw a figure scuttling toward him. His hand tightened on the hilt of his knife, but when he recognized her he relaxed.

"Corina!" he shouted, and he was beside himself with joy to see her safe.

She ran to him. He could see the fear in her eyes and he heard it in her voice. "Oh, Lucio! They came looking for your pearl after you were gone."

"Who?" he asked.

"I didn't see. It was all darkness when they came into the house. I climbed through the window to escape when I heard them enter, and I hid in the brush." She saw the intensity in his face. "They looked everywhere inside. They tore the house apart, but they didn't find it. They didn't get the pearl, Lucio. I heard their words, the anger in their voices when they left my house."

"You have it then?" he asked eagerly. "The pearl?"

"It is still in the house where I hid it." She caught her breath.

Lucio took the lead. "Come," he said.

"What will you do now, Lucio?"

"First let us get the pearl and then we will decide on a course of action."

When they returned to the house neither Heléna or Ernesto were there. In her room Corina looked at the place where her bed had been. Everything was pulled apart. Her mattress was torn and her clothing scattered about. Even the little religious altar on the shelf, with a serene statue of the Holy Virgin and the devotional candles that she kept burning, had been pulled down.

She went to the far wall and found the place on the floor. The boards there were covered by the drip of candle wax. The accumulation over the years had formed a thick pattern of ridges and valleys. Carefully she examined the area and then she used her fingers to pry away a nearly perfect square section of the floor. It was her secret hiding place that even her mother didn't know. It was here that Corina kept her private treasures -- a flower Lucio once had given her, now dried and preserved, a picture of a beautiful movie actress from an American Hollywood magazine, the book where she wrote her poems and where she kept the list of her hopes and her dreams.

She looked into the dark, hollow space and felt inside with her hand. She reached deep into the opening and pulled out the pearl. Then she replaced the wax-covered board, and the hiding place disappeared as though it had never existed.

She went back to Lucio and presented him with his pearl. "Here is your precious pearl," she said. "And now what is your plan?"

The relief showed on Lucio's face. He had been certain that it was lost, and now he was relieved to hold it in his hands again. As he looked into the smooth surface for the answer to her question he was again hypnotized by the great pearl's beauty. But what he saw was chaos and confusion. He knew one thing, that he must sell the pearl quickly and claim his rightful fortune before it was taken away. There were other thoughts in his head -- the body of Clementé in the brush, the injured Ernesto, all those things that Lucio wanted and soon would be able to buy, his marriage to Corina.

The weight of her words made the pearl heavier in his hand. "I am confused," he said. "I will go into La Paz, to the church, and pray for divine guidance. I will go and see the old priest. Maybe he can help take away the curse that is here," he said finally.

"Then I will go with you," Corina said. And when Lucio protested, he could not dissuade her. "Lucio," she said calmly, "our future and the pearl are one and the same. I want to be with you. We will go into the city together."

And that was what they did. Corina followed Lucio, and together they stepped into the morning light.

It was the beginning of another day.

Chapter Six

The old priest was seated in the kitchen of the rectory. He was finishing the last of his breakfast, a soft-boiled egg from the dozen fresh eggs brought to him as an offering. The Indian who had delivered them still warm that morning had no money to petition a favor from God, and he knew that such things cost. Although the man might have traded the eggs or sold them, fed them to his own children, he had hoped that the little gift to the priest might influence the holy father to speed the man's petition before God.

"Cast your bread on the waters," the priest had often preached in his sermons, "and it will return a hundred-fold." That lesson, he was happy to note, seemed also to apply to eggs.

The priest chewed the last piece of bacon, also a donation for a baptism he had performed, from a family who couldn't afford to pay the stipend for his services. He dipped his bread, baked this morning by his housekeeper, into the golden yolk and savored the flavor. He licked his soft fingers clean, and he wiped them on the hem inside his dusty black robe.

He had been planning to take the long walk from the church down into the village, before the sun was too hot for *civilized* people to be about in the streets. He thought to find out the new owner of the great pearl and to remind him of the debt he owed to God for such good fortune. When he heard a soft rustling behind him, he turned to see his housekeeper standing silently in the doorway.

"*Pardon, Padre*," she said in Spanish, lowering her eyes. This woman, who had taken care of the priest for more years than she could count, fixing his meals, cleaning his house, washing and repairing his soiled clothing, knew him as intimately as any wife knows her husband. She was aware of his secrets, his annoying habits and his shortcomings. Yet, she maintained her deep respect and great wonderment for someone so close to God, someone who could forgive sin with the simple wave of his hand, who could perform the miracle of changing bread and wine into the body and blood of Christ. She was in awe of this man who had the ear of God, and spoke directly to the Holy Virgin and the saints. "There are two Indians at the door," she said barely above a whisper. "A young man and a girl. They wish to speak with you."

The priest was a little annoyed at this unexpected interruption of his plans and it showed on his face. But he nodded curtly and dismissed the woman who retreated with a small bow to show them in.

In another moment the housekeeper led Lucio, followed by Corina, into the kitchen. The smell of fried bacon and baked bread, still hanging in the smoky morning air, made Lucio's empty stomach rumble loud enough to be heard in the quiet room.

The priest wiped his hands again and he forced a smiled, but his old blue eyes didn't smile. He took in these two young Indians at a glance, adding the sum of their parts, the condition of Lucio's torn clothes, his dirty hands, and his bruises. He assessed Corina's open-mouthed wonder, her simple dress, and he dismissed them immediately as charity cases.

"*Padre*," Lucio began respectfully, "we have come to ask you-"

"My house keeper will give you some food," the priest interrupted impatiently. "But there is no money," he said more sternly. He was intent on making short work of them and getting on with his more pressing business of the day.

"It isn't your food we want," Lucio said with an edge in his voice that was unmistakable. "Or your money." He wouldn't be put off and dismissed like a child. "We have come to you with a problem."

The priest looked at the sad eyes of this pretty young woman and he concluded that she was probably pregnant, that they were there for him to perform a quick wedding ceremony to spare the embarrassment of her parents, and to save her reputation in the village. The deep creases of a frown cut into the priest's face. No matter how many sermons he delivered against the sins of the flesh, these unrepentant people continued to surrender to the temptations of the Devil. Like the animals that they raised, they were content to live their short, wretched lives in squalor, work and breed the new generations to follow in their sordid footsteps. Like lustful children, they were unable to control their lower instincts.

"If it's a wedding that you want, you will have to come back another time. I am too busy today with *important* matters. I have no time for you." He stared at Corina's slender waist, wondering how far along she might be. "Besides," he added with some contempt that he did not try to hide, "your secret will be safe for a while yet. From the looks of this girl, you still have time before her pregnancy begins to show."

His words were like a slap in the face to Corina, who blushed deeply and covered her embarrassment in her hands. Likewise, it was an insult to Lucio. But he would not be silent.

"She in *not* pregnant!" he said with anger that exploded from within. "We *will* be married when the time is right! But that is not why we have come to you today." He reached under his shirt and he produced the piece of leather. He opened it carefully and the pearl rolled into the palm of his dirty hand. "Perhaps I have made a big mistake coming to you at all."

The unexpected vision of such a pearl took the breath away from the old priest, and he fell back into his chair with a groan. What he saw was beyond his thinking, greater than his wildest imaginings. This pearl was larger than the chicken egg he had consumed, and perfect in every respect. He had heard from those who brought the news that the pearl was the greatest La Paz had ever seen. They had called it the "Pearl of the

World." But hardly did the priest expect it would be *such* a pearl. The priest could barely keep himself from reaching out and plucking it from Lucio's hand.

He sank back into his chair and when he finally found breath enough to speak, his words took a condescending tone that wasn't missed by Lucio. "I am sorry, my son, if I may have seemed impatient. But I was in a hurry to visit a sick man and give him absolution before he is called before the Heavenly Father. However," he said with his eyes not leaving the pearl, "I can see that you are in some deep distress. I will listen, and maybe I can provide some assistance." He used the edge of the table to help him to his feet and he came closer to Lucio. "Glory to Him who has created such a thing of beauty."

The priest waved his fingers in the air in front of them as a small benediction over Lucio and Corina and then he blessed himself. They made the Sign of the Cross, kissing their fingers up to heaven.

"But how could a man who has such a wonderful pearl possibly have problems?" the priest asked. "God has been more than generous to you, my son. I hope you will remember Him who has given you such a great blessing." It sounded like the words he delivered from the pulpit at the Sunday morning Mass.

"I will," Lucio said closing his hand over the pearl. "I gave God my solemn promise to donate–" He remembered what he had promised to God, but Lucio considered carefully his words to the priest. "–some of the money to the church when I have sold it. And then Corina and I will be married, at a Solemn High Mass, and have a big *fiesta* in La Paz's finest hotel."

The priest smiled when he heard the words and so did Corina, her face flushing with excitement. "Those are good thoughts," he said. "But what is the problem that brings you here this morning?"

"This pearl," Lucio said, "has brought only bad luck to me and much pain to my friends. Some say it is cursed, and now I am afraid it may be so." Lucio told him the details of everything that had happened. "In less than a day I have been attacked twice.

Once in the night men came into my house, and in defense I wounded a man." The death of Clementé was something he would save for his confession. "And then on the road I was beaten and left for dead. Now my house has been burned to the ground and everything in Corina's house has been destroyed. Those who want this pearl are willing to take it from me at any price."

The priest clucked his tongue to show his concern, shaking his gray head and comforting the crying Corina with gentle pats. All the time he stared at the beauty of the pearl that was in Lucio's hand.

When Lucio finished his story, the priest thought for a moment and then he said, "It is the Devil who has found his way into this pearl and means to use it to find his way into the hearts of men. But I am sure that I can help. We will go together into the church and I will offer my prayers to God to cast out the Devil. I will ask that the Lord place your pearl under His divine protection and that of the angels and the saints. Juan!" he called.

A man appeared suddenly in the doorway. Lucio slipped the pearl under his shirt for safekeeping as he came into the room. "Yes, *Padre*," the man said, holding his hat in his hands.

"This is the one you told me of who has found the great pearl. Now I am going with them to the church for a blessing. But there are some important matters I want you to attend when I am gone." The priest whispered and the man nodded and stared at Lucio, who felt uneasy under his gaze.

"Yes, *Padre*. As you say," the man nodded again and rushed out through the door of the rectory.

"Now come with me," the priest said and he slowly led the way to the church.

The hierarchy of beggars was already at their customary post in front of the church doors. They were the old, the infirm, the mothers with young children, and the frail, dirty orphans who spent their nights in the streets. Those who were lucky enough slept in cardboard boxes. Begging was their profession. It was their life, to sit and watch and to wait for the generosity of others. One old man sat nodding in half-sleep with his back against the stone church wall and his hat turned up on his knees, ready to accept the morning's donations. The beggars watched with great interest the approach of Lucio and Corina, estimating their worth and calculating the amount of the donation they could afford. They were expert in such matters, as they studied the manner in which Lucio was dressed, Corina's age, and they dismissed the pair as poor Indians, hardly worth their attention.

The old priest scattered the beggars like chickens, tossing a handful of blessings like feed corn. He pulled open the church door and the faint aroma of incense rushed out to greet them as they entered. It was a familiar scent that brought Lucio back to his childhood when he had sometimes served as an altar boy for this very priest. It was a smell that made him feel safe and uneasy at the same time. It mingled with Lucio's memories of the years gone, of countless Masses and weddings, and of funerals.

Inside the church was dark and noticeably cooler than the outside air. A few people, mostly women dressed in black, sat in the empty pews. They were the holdovers from the early morning Mass. An old woman, her head covered with a tattered shawl, fingered her rosary silently mouthing Hail Marys as she counted the beads. Another woman slowly made her way along the perimeter of the church, marking the suffering journey of Jesus in the Stations of the Cross.

The old priest dipped his finger into the holy water and Lucio and Corina followed his lead. He genuflected with some difficulty as he crossed himself and the crack of his old knees sounded like a shot in the silence of the church. The priest brought them away from praying lips and prying eyes, to the side altar where they would be alone.

"First we will ask God," the priest said, "to remove any curse that may be on your pearl. And then, in the name of Christ, we will cast out the Devil that is in this pearl."

He took the gold plate that was used to hold the consecrated bread and he presented it to Lucio. "Place your pearl here and we will offer it to God."

Lucio removed the pearl from its wrapping and reluctantly he placed it on the plate, out of his reach and out of his control. The priest's hands trembled, and the pearl rolled in a slow circle along the golden edge and then it settled into the depression at the center. The beauty of the pearl was re-doubled by its gold reflection. Its surface caught a shaft of sunlight that sliced through a broken pane in the stained glass window and sent it back toward Heaven.

"When do you plan to sell this pearl?" the priest asked with a strained indifference, as though trying to make idle conversation.

"Soon. Maybe today, when I go to the pearl buyers." Lucio looked uneasily at the shadows around the church.

"And what do you think its value will be?"

"It is hard to say," Lucio replied. He was annoyed at the priest's concern for such material matters and suddenly he wasn't sure that being there was a good idea. He was anxious to leave. "No one has ever seen such a pearl, and no one can know what price it will bring."

Then a small sound came from behind them and Lucio turned. He saw a dark figure drop back into the shadows. His attention returned to the priest who raised his eyes to heaven and began to pray. He held the gold plate in his hands and extended it above his head. The pearl once again rolled around the edge.

"There," the priest said when he was finished reciting the magic words in the strange language that belonged to God and to his priests, "I have removed the curse for you. And I have blessed this marvelous pearl with an extra prayer to make it and its owner safe. Now your pearl is under the protection of God and his saints."

Lucio heard the scuttle of feet on the stone floor. He whirled around in time to see one man running toward him, and another figure carrying a wooden club coming from the left. Lucio snatched the pearl from the plate that fell from the priest's shaking hands and clattered to the altar floor. At the same time he pulled his machete from under his shirt where he had kept it hidden.

"No!" the priest yelled. "Violence in the House of God is a sacrilege!"

But Lucio was in motion. He met the attack of the first man by hitting him on the side of the head, using the flat side of the heavy blade like a club. The force of the blow echoed off the stone and it sent his attacker to the cool floor. The man's head made a thud when he fell and his breath caught in his throat like a death rattle. Then Lucio, his eyes intense and fierce, turned with his machete at the ready to face the second attacker. From deep inside him some animal sound broke free as Lucio advanced on the other man, whose desire to fight was now clearly gone. The man stopped and he threw down the club. He retreated slowly, backing away from Lucio's advance and searching for some place of escape. Then he turned and fled quickly through the side door of the church.

Lucio grabbed Corina's hand. "Come," he said, and they broke for the door at the back.

The startled priest called after them. "But what about your promise to God?" he asked. "What about the offering?"

"We will return," Lucio tossed back with anger. He was still holding his machete. "Then I will settle my affairs with God, and then I will settle with *you*."

They ran quickly, stopping only long enough to genuflect and bless themselves with holy water before they fled into the city.

Chapter Seven

The beggars were deep into weaving the sad stories of their own private tragedies for the growing crowd of *touristas* in front of the church, too involved to notice the commotion. They barely raised their eyes when Corina and Lucio, still holding his machete, raced quickly from the church and into the street clogged with the big American cars driven down from the border. Some of the tourists wandering through La Paz seemed startled by the sight of two young Indians running armed through the streets. But they attributed it to some or another strange native custom, some curious Indian ritual and snapped pictures before continuing on a quest for other photo opportunities, more quaint shops and incredible bargains to take back home with them.

Lucio's heart was beating fast. He was always frightened and uneasy in the city. The hot paving stones under his sandals felt hard and unnatural. The tall buildings pressed in on him and made it difficult for him to breathe. Whenever he went into the city, no matter how many times he was there, he had a sense of walking on unfamiliar ground. And now, with Corina at his side and his pearl tucked away under his shirt, he could feel the staring eyes of strangers, the chilling fear of being watched from every window, from every shadowed doorway. It felt as though the eyes boring into his back looked through to his soul. He didn't need to turn around to confirm his feeling. Some animal thing in Lucio, the instinct that long ago lived in his people, told him he was being followed as they wound their way through the maze of streets and back alleys.

"Did you recognize the man in the church?" Corina asked when she caught her breath. "Was he the one who attacked you in the night?"

"I can not say. I did not see who attacked me in the night," Lucio said, stealing a quick look back over his shoulder. "But the second man in the church, the one who ran away, he might have been the man who worked for the priest. But I can not be certain even of that."

"You do not believe that the priest would try to steal the pearl? He is a man of God. Surely the priest can be trusted," she said.

"I do not trust anyone," Lucio said. In the short time that he had this pearl he had learned that *every* man might be his enemy. And now Lucio had to be on guard for everything, for everyone. "Not even the priest."

Her eyes were full of the fear that she felt for both of them. "Now where will we go, Lucio? What will we do?"

"We have only one choice. We will go quickly now, directly to where the pearl buyers keep their offices." He changed direction and disappeared into a narrow alley and then he cut back again. "We must get to the pearl buyers and sell this pearl now, before it is lost, before it is taken."

Lucio picked up the pace, tightening his grip on Corina's hand pulling her behind him. And together they made their way through the city.

* * *

Every day the pearl buyers waited in their offices, where they practiced looking bored and unconcerned, until the Indian pearl fishers came to them with their pearls. But today it was different. Although it did not show on the faces of these men, who were experts in the art of haggling and indifference, there was a sense of excitement that hung in the air. They had heard the accounts of a great pearl and they were eager to see it and to possess it.

These buyers expended little effort of their own and they produced nothing of value. They did no work and still they grew rich, off the work of others. And because business was good for them, they were never concerned with thoughts about their next meal. They always ate well and had grown soft and fat. In La Paz, where pearls had always been a way of life, the pearl buyers were thought to be the masters, who controlled a fisher's destiny by setting the artificial and arbitrary price a pearl would bring. But these pearl buyers, who sat in their offices day after day, were themselves slaves to the pearls and, in some deep ironic way, to the very fishers who found them. The comfortable lives to which the buyers had grown accustomed were fragile and rested in the callused hands of those who risked death to take the pearls from the sea. A pearl buyer with no skills and no pearls to buy would certainly starve.

In the waters of the Sea of Cortez there are small fish called remoras that swim in the company of the larger fish. The remoras have a sucking disk on the head with which they attach themselves to the hulls of ships, whales, sea turtles, or sharks. Oblivious to their own peril, they live their entire lives under the dangerous, cold eyes of predators, taking some protection from them, settling for the scraps of food that fall from the jaws of their hosts. For some unknown reason, the big fish tolerate the little fish that swim about unmolested, and both predator and remora seem to thrive in their symbiotic relationship.

So it was in La Paz, where the buyers were the sharks, gobbling up large profits from the sale of the pearls and the Indian divers were the little fish living on what was left for them. But only the pearl buyers understood this. And the Indians, because they didn't comprehend the power that they might wield if the they united, were content to accept only the meager share, the scraps offered them for all their efforts.

All of the pearl buyers were stingy with what they paid the fishers. But always they managed to turn the pearls they bought into great profits for themselves, by selling them at greatly inflated prices to a growing market of rich *Americanos* who were drawn to La Paz in search of a bargain. These buyers were students of human nature. They knew that vanity in a person is a curious thing. One might easily walk past a starving beggar in the streets without a thought of tossing him a single *peso*. But to adorn a manicured finger or to grace an elegant neck, that same person would think nothing of throwing away a fortune for a pearl, an oddity of Nature formed by an oyster in a desperate act of self-defense. The buyers relied on this vanity in their customers and they courted it. And preyed on it, just as they preyed on the continued ignorance of the poor fishermen who came daily to their offices.

Once, a long time ago, before the buyers had become so corrupt, the different shops were places of competition for the many men who bid wildly on a fisher's pearls. But now in La Paz, the buyers had formed a syndicate, a consortium, as a means of consolidating their power. They did this by a secret understanding among the buyers to fix the price of pearls and avoid the needless competition of bidding too high and cutting their profits. An individual dealer had learned that it was better to lose a single pearl, letting it go to another for a lower amount, than to drive up the price of what was paid for all pearls in the frenzy to own *every* pearl. If they were not too greedy, they knew, there was enough money to be made by everyone, except perhaps for the unsuspecting divers.

Of course the buyers had heard the news about the great pearl. There are few secrets in a small town, and for those they paid. They knew that it was just a matter of time before its owner brought it to them for appraisal. For a pearl, no matter how large and perfect, is in reality merely a trinket. For all its beauty, a hungry man cannot eat his pearl and a pearl will not keep him and his family warm on the chilly nights.

One buyer sat patiently in his office. He knew that the Indian who had found such a great pearl, "The Pearl of the World" according to his informants, planned to sell it that very day. It was just a matter of time before he found his way to where the buyers kept their offices. Of course the buyer hoped that he would have an opportunity to bid on it and own it for the lowest price, but he also realized that such an outcome was, among other things, a matter of luck. And he whispered a silent prayer to that end.

The man marked the progress of the day as he watched the shadow of a building, like a giant sundial, creep slowly across the street in front of his office. With the blade of a small pearl handled knife he carefully pared the cuticles of his hands, accentuating and enlarging the half moon of each nail. He let the remnants of dead skin collect on his desktop before he blew them off and swept the rest away with the back of his hand. Then with a pad he kept in his desk drawer he buffed the nails to a glossy pink sheen and admired them. He barely stifled a yawn with a soft, fat hand and picked at a speck of lint that clung to his white linen suit.

Particles of dust hanging in the warm air danced lazily in the almost still sunlight. The sweet smoke of his hand-rolled Cuban cigar burning in a sterling silver ashtray on the buyer's desk spiraled up like a thin gray string and was reflected in the ornately framed mirror that hung on the wall across the room. The smoke mingled with the fine particles of dust, until the air in the office was all dust and smoke and mirror.

He took the cigar and rolled it between his fingers and admired the ash tip. He sucked on the cigar, as he dreamed of what might be done with the profits from the pearl, if he was the one to get it. He pictured the cruise ships that daily steamed into the estuary of La Paz and he considered how good it would be to send away his wife and his children for a long vacation in California. That would afford him time and the opportunity to explore his "other interests" while they were away, something he had not been able to do for a while. And his mind went to the many beautiful young women he knew in La Paz.

A sound from outside brought the man out of his daydream and to attention. Without thinking he formed his face into a practiced smile for the two people who came into his office. His lips parted showing his straight teeth, but the man's eyes were cold and piercing like the eyes of a hawk.

"Good morning," he said. He looked at the swinging pendulum of the old Regulator clock that ticked and reverberated like a heartbeat from the wall. "Or is it good afternoon?" Although he didn't know this Indian's name, he recognized Lucio as one of the pearl fishers who sometimes came into his office. "And what can I do for you, my friend, on this fine day?" He rose from behind his desk to greet them as they entered.

"I have a pearl I hope to sell," Lucio said simply, his careless tone indicating neither his concern nor his stress.

"Well, my friend, that is why I am here. To buy pearls. Or else I would shut my office and move my family to Mexico City, where the climate is better and where the people have more money to spend," he laughed at his joke, but Lucio did not smile. Seeing this, the buyer switched moods as smoothly as a driver switches gears and the expression on the buyer's face changed to one of sincerity and concern. He was a chameleon, able to assume many shades. "You have come to the right place, my friend. We have done business before, you and I. And I have always treated you generously and with respect." He looked at Corina and he smiled. "In all of La Paz," he said more for her, "no one will give you a better price. Let me see these pearls of yours and I will give you the *best* price." He sat back in his chair.

"I have just *one* pearl," Lucio said with a pride he couldn't hide. "The most wonderful pearl ever taken from the waters of La Paz."

And then the buyer knew that his prayers had been answered and wish had come true. He grew anxious, but he didn't want Lucio to see his anxiety. He lifted his cigar and puffed casually until the gray ash tip glowed red and then cooled. He examined the smooth burn of the tobacco leaf and enjoyed the aroma, while he balled his other hand into a fist to keep it from shaking. He watched as Lucio reached under his shirt and produced the leather wrap.

The man had laid an empty black velvet lined tray on the countertop and Lucio dropped the pearl into it. All the time Lucio's eyes were fixed on the face of the dealer for any hint of emotion that might indicate the true value of his pearl and what price he might expect from the buyer. But the man was an expert and he held his features like a mask. Only his smile changed, to a look of disappointment and then to one of pity. A derisive snorting sound escaped from the buyer.

When he turned to Lucio he was shaking his head. "It is a *very* large pearl," he said.

"No one has ever found a larger one in all of La Paz," Lucio was quick to respond.

The buyer chuckled. "Perhaps." He looked from Lucio to Corina and formed his face into a grin. "As with many other things in life, size isn't the only factor to be considered. How *big* a thing is often is not so important." There was no mistaking his suggestive meaning. The buyer's words made Corina blush and brought a scowl to Lucio's face, which caused the buyer again to switch gears. "And so," he said, carefully measuring his words, "it is the same with pearls, where the *quality* counts most in determining its value."

Casually he picked up the pearl and tested it between his thumb and forefinger, measuring it, squeezing it all around as a child might test a piece of candy before popping it into the mouth, which Lucio half expected he might do that next. The man pursed his lips until they were a thin line and almost disappeared below his mustache. Then he took the large pearl handled magnifying glass that he kept on the desk and he examined the pearl closely for a long time under the light of his lamp. From across the desk Corina marveled at the size of the man's eye behind the lens and she might have laughed if she had not felt the tension coming from Lucio.

"I'm sorry, my friend," the buyer said after a careful study. "As you have said, it is a big pearl. But I'm afraid it is not a very *good* pearl."

His words knocked the air out of Lucio, like a sudden punch in the stomach and it made his knees buckle. "It is the 'Pearl of the World'!" he protested.

The buyer shook his head and looked at him with pity, as a parent might pity a child. "There is a serious defect," he spoke softly, "deep inside this pearl at the center. At its heart. Like a cancer growing in a young body that will someday be the cause of death, this flaw has already killed your pearl. It has marred its beauty and lowered its value. On the surface this pearl may seem fine to an untrained eye, but I can tell you that it has grown around a core that is hollow and rotten. Just from its size alone one can see that this pearl has been too long under the water, my friend. Its center is spongy. And it is just a matter of time before your *'Pearl of the World*' loses all of its life and crumbles to dust."

Lucio was confused. He looked to Corina for support, but the dealer's words had shaken her as well. Before they had entered the office, her head danced with the dreams of marriage and a happy, comfortable life with her husband Lucio. But those dreams were now scattered like a flock of startled pigeons in the market square. She read the confusion in Lucio's eyes and she could not help him.

"But, my friend," the dealer said, "don't just take my word for it. You can take your pearl and visit all the dealers in the square. And they will tell you just what I have said. Then after you have seen them, if you want, come back and I will see what I can do to make a deal with you." His words were a dismissal, and the man sat back in his chair and puffed his cigar. And then a thought seemed to come to him. "Better still," he said, "I can save you the trouble and have the other buyers come here to you, and then you will see for yourself. Carlos!" he called without giving Lucio a chance to respond.

A thin young boy with frightened eyes pushed through the beaded curtains in the back and came into the office. The boy, holding his head down, avoided looking at Lucio's still puzzled face.

"Carlos," the buyer ordered, "go to *Senor* Lopez and to *Senor* Ortega across the square. Tell them, as a courtesy to me, I would ask them to close up their offices for a short time and come here to me. I have an old pearl that I want them to value. Tell them that I have set no price yet and that I want the owner to consider several offers before he agrees to the sale."

"Yes, *patron*," the boy nodded and he hurried past Lucio and Corina on his way into the square.

When he was gone the dealer turned his full attention back to Lucio. "Even before they come," he said, "before they make you any offer on this pearl, I can offer you say–" He counted on his fingers and made some calculations on a small slip of paper. "– ten thousand *pesos* for it. Then I will try to sell it, unload it on some unsuspecting *gringo* tourist. And if I am lucky I may even make a modest profit." He smiled kindly, but his eyes were not kind. They were as cold as ice. He gestured with his hand that was holding the cigar, curling a ribbon of smoke into the air. "Reselling that pearl would barely pay my rent for a week. My friend, you have no idea the expenses I have to meet, the overhead to maintain this office. A family to feed. A complaining wife to keep happy." He nodded his head resignedly. "But I am sure you know how troublesome a women can be at times."

Lucio wasn't listening. "*Ten thousand pesos*?" he said in disbelief. "This pearl is worth ten hundred thousand!" But deep inside Lucio wasn't sure. Perhaps this buyer was right. Lucio had taken the pearl from the water and not from an oyster. There was no telling how long it had been in the sand. And ten thousand *was* a great deal of money, more money than Lucio had ever had at one time, or ever hoped to have. There certainly were many things he could do with it.

Adding to Lucio's confusion, the dealer went to his cash drawer and he pulled out a pile of old bills as an incentive and he waved them casually in the air. "It is a handsome sum of money, my friend. With ten thousand *pesos* a man might make *one* woman *very* happy." He laughed and turned to Corina again. The expression on his face made her shiver. "Or if he chooses, a man can make *many* women a *little* happy, if you take my meaning. In any event, ten thousand *pesos* will buy enough tequila that a man may stay drunk for a long time, with or without a woman."

The confusion in Lucio's head cleared, and his strength and his resolve returned. He snatched his pearl from the black velvet tray. "No!" he said. "You are a liar! My pearl is not for sale. I will not be cheated by you."

The buyer looked hurt. "My friend, your words are an insult," the buyer said, and his face showed his surprise. "But because I understand your disappointment, I will not be offended, my friend. But *you* must understand this. I am a businessman. If I cheat my clients, it would not make for good business and I would not be in business for very long. I know you expected more, but there is sometimes a wide gulf between our heightened expectations and reality. There is nothing I can do to change that. Do not be so hasty to react. After all, I am not the one to blame for this imperfection in your pearl," he said sadly. "I feel that I must tell you, because you are a man with whom I have done business before, you are making a big mistake if you do not sell. Hold on to this pearl and it will disintegrate before your eyes in a month, in a week. And then you will have nothing to show for your efforts." He paused to let his words sink in. "But if you still think I am lying, my friend, just wait until the other dealers come and you will see for yourself. I can guarantee that you will get no better offer than mine in all of La Paz."

"In La Paz, perhaps." Lucio was furious and it was his anger that made him talk. "But La Paz is not the world. There are other places, other cities I can take my pearl. I-" he stammered until he found the words, "-I would rather *donate* my pearl to the old priest in the church, or give it to the beggars who sit in front of the church. I would take more satisfaction if I destroyed it. I would first crush it between two rocks rather than be cheated here." Lucio wrapped the pearl with resolve and stashed it under his shirt.

"Wait!" the dealer said. "I can see that you are a passionate man. And I am a fool, I know. The other pearl buyers will laugh at my foolishness when they come and they hear what I have done. But because I value your business, my friend, and because I hope to continue doing business with you in the future," he reached into his cash drawer again, "I will pay you *fifteen thousand pesos* for this poor pearl, and make no profit when I sell it. I would even be willing to suffer a loss, just to restore your faith in me and to keep your continued trust." He held the money out toward Lucio.

Corina looked from the handful of bills to Lucio. Although it was not the fortune he had hoped for, fifteen thousand *pesos* would still be more than enough money to be married and to set up Lucio's house with the things they would need to start their family. It was all that Corina could do not to snatch the money from the hand of the buyer, and she hoped that the proud and stubborn Lucio would consent. She prayed that he would.

But Lucio was already at the door. His face was red with the rage that he felt. His head pounded and his eyes were blurred with his anger. He glared at the boy Carlos and the two stout men who were entering the office. When they blocked his escape in the doorway he pushed through them. And Corina followed in his wake.

"But what about these others?" the dealer called. "Let them at least see your pearl and tender an offer-"

But the door swung shut with a slam of irrevocable finality.

The dealer took a long puff on his cigar and he watched as the hot ash dropped from the tip to the top of his desk, where it glowed and burned black into the shining waxed finish. He shook his head at the two surprised men. He had played the game to the best of his ability. "I tried," he said. "I had hoped it would go more easily. But this man is too stubborn. He would not even consider my most generous offer. He has threatened that he will give his pearl to the church, or destroy it. He said that he will take his business elsewhere. Away from La Paz," he added sadly to the confused men. "So now, I am afraid that the matter is out of our hands."

With his right foot he pressed a secret button that was under his desk and a light flashed in the back room of his office. It was the pre-arranged signal to one who was waiting there, a signal that the deal had gone wrong.

Chapter Eight

Lucio waited in the cool shadow of the crowded street. His face was hot and he was perspiring. His mind was confused, clouded by the rage and the frustration that he felt. Not so many days ago he was a happy man and just yesterday he was a rich man. His good fortune seemed to assure his wellbeing, body and soul, with the promise of money enough that he would never again want for anything in his life. All that Lucio hoped was to get a fair price for his pearl, to keep his promises to God and to live the remaining days of his life in relative peace and comfort. But now all that seemed to be slipping through his battered fingers.

In his anger and his haste he had told the pearl buyer that he would give his pearl away, that he would even leave the village rather than be cheated. Saying so was the same as doing so. Now there was no choice left to him but to do as he had said he would. To surrender to this injustice, to go back on his word was to be less than a man. But the thought of leaving the comfort and the familiarity of La Paz was even more frightening than facing those who had come after him in the night. He was in a trap that he had fashioned with his own words and now he must be true to those words, or lose face.

Once, he knew very well, his grandfather Kino had made such a stand, and it had cost him dearly. Lucio recalled his father's words, "Kino paid a high price for his honor," he had said many times, with great pride in his eyes and in his voice. "His house was burned to the ground. A hole was broken in his boat, this very one we sail. And the life of his first child, Coyotito, my brother, was lost. But always, even in his great loss, Kino was a man to be reckoned with. *Always he was a man.* Kino was defiant to the end, when he threw his pearl into the sea. Whatever else they took, they could not take from him his honor or his pride. Never!"

Corina saw the deep lines of concern cut into Lucio's face, but she did not dare to speak. She remained quiet for a long time. When she finally did speak she did so quietly and she picked her words carefully. She knew what she was about to say would hurt him, and she did not want to add any further injury to what Lucio had already suffered.

"Lucio," she began gently, "I know how difficult it has been for you. You have said that your pearl is not for sale here in La Paz and that you would take it to another place to get a better price. I know that by saying it you now feel you must do so. But, Lucio, this pearl is less than nothing to me and you are everything. Now I am afraid for you. I'm afraid that you will leave and I will never see you again because you will be killed. Lucio, I am afraid for *us*. Please consider the fifteen thousand *pesos*. It is such a fortune. More money than you could hope to make even if you filled your boat with fish every day for a year. If you take the pearl buyer's offer, we can still be married and-"

"Quiet!" he cautioned her fiercely, as some of the anger that he felt spilled onto her. "I will not be cheated by anyone. I will not give up my dreams. And I will not have my dreams taken away. To give in to those cheats is an affront to me and to the memory of Kino. But when I succeed, it will be a vindication for him. For all that he suffered and for all that he lost."

Moving cautiously in the shadows he watched the people around them, studying the faces to see who might be an enemy, who might try to take his pearl. But they were the faces of strangers, city people, street venders with the trinkets that they hoped to unload on the loud *gringos* who were already out in force. Again Lucio's head began to spin. He felt dizzy and disoriented. The noise made him on edge and he was unable to breathe, as though the crowd passing around them had taken all the air from his lungs.

They were half way across the plaza when he stopped and turned around. Lucio saw the men. There were two of them standing at the end of the alley near the pearl buyer's office, engaged in what seemed to be casual conversation. But something about them wasn't right. When they saw Lucio staring at them, the men tensed and looked uneasy. Although Lucio didn't recognize them, his instinct told him that they were dangerous. It was clear to him why they were there. They would follow him and Corina and when the end came, if he still had the pearl in his possession, they would try to take it from him. Or if he had sold it, they would try to take his money.

Lucio gripped Corina's arm firmly and they changed their direction again, heading further into the crowd and the confusion of the streets that made up the city. He said nothing to her. He didn't want to frighten Corina, but already there was fear in her eyes. She had seen them too.

"Lucio," she said, "those men were watching us."

"Yes," he answered. "I know. I saw them. But they are behind us now, and maybe we can lose them." He turned to see if they were following and Lucio's eyes squinted into the bright sunlight. But the men had blended into the shadows and into the crowd. Even if he eluded them, Lucio knew, there would be others. He knew that they would not give up their pursuit until they had what they wanted, until they or he or all of them were dead.

Corina was even more frightened now because she could see that Lucio was afraid. She could feel the tension in his body as his muscles contracted. She could hear his breathing became shallow and quick. "What do we do now, Lucio?" she asked, relying on him for some direction.

"Perhaps if we split up," he said. "You go back to your family, where you will be safe. I will get to my boat and set sail to the north. If I can get to another town, maybe Loreto, I will sell the pearl there. Then, when I return with the money, we will be married as I have promised."

"But I want to stay with you," she said. "We can fight them together. Alone, I am afraid you will be killed. There are two of them. If you face them by yourself–" She left her thought unfinished and turned to face him. "I *will* to stay with you."

"No!" Lucio said. "You will do as I say!" He grabbed her roughly and held her by the arms until they hurt. The pressure from his fingers left a bruise on her skin. Although it was his hands that hurt her, it was his anger that stung Corina more, like the pinch of a scorpion or the bite of a snake. And then Lucio released his hold and his tone softened. He touched her cheek softly and looked into her dark, frightened eyes. "I am sorry, Corina. Already I have put you in too much danger. Besides, I can go faster without you. When I return from selling the pearl we will be together. It is my pledge to you."

Corina wanted to argue, but she knew it was not the time to do so. His mind was made up and he would not even hear anything else she had to say. Lucio was a man, and a man, Corina knew, was stubborn and proud. She knew that sometimes a man could be very foolish, saying and doing things without considering the consequences of his words. It was a woman's part to keep her man from harm because of his foolishness. She had often heard her mother laughing and talking with the other women in the village. Heléna had said it many times to her young daughter as well, "A man sees a door that is closed and he is ready to throw all his weight, his power and his strength against it to open it. He will run and smash himself into the door until he knocks it down, or until he knocks himself out! Men," she said without hostility, but with deep understanding, "are like little children. They have room in their simple minds for only one thought at a time. It is up to a woman to point out that perhaps the door isn't locked and all a man need do to pass through is simply turn the handle."

There was humor in Heléna's little story, but Corina knew there also was wisdom and truth. She would do as Lucio said, for now, but she would use her woman's mind to think of a way to help him out of his problem. Maybe in her woman's heart she could turn the handle and unlock the door. Maybe she could find a solution that Lucio and his man's mind could not see.

Lucio picked up the pace of his steps and he led Corina by the arm, directly into the heart of the La Paz. As they began their flight, Lucio felt a prickling in the back of his neck, as though some animal instinct came alive in him. It came to him on his fear, yet it went beyond fear. This was a vestige of the primitive past, the animal part of man, long dormant, which once was so strong in the human species. It was a force so powerful that it enabled frail humanity not just to survive, but to thrive over those that were bigger and stronger and fiercer. It bubbled up from a deep well inside Lucio, from a place and a time when living depended on cunning and inner personal strength. It was this instinct that took over Lucio, making him tense and, at the same time, making him calm. Now fully awakened, it alerted all of his senses.

Together Lucio and Corina made their way into the growing crowd of people. And at a distance the two men followed them.

What no one saw was a third man, a dark figure who stepped from the shadows of the pearl buyer's office. His hard face was etched by a scar, the remnants of an old knife wound that started at his left eyebrow, ran down his cheek and chin and cut across his throat to the base of his right ear. It gave the impression that the man's face was a mask that could be peeled away in one piece.

At a glance the man appraised the situation, and his cruel, dark eyes smiled. He was a patient man. He would let the other two do the dirty work and then he would simply step in and relieve them of the pearl, or the money if the pearl was sold. Either way it didn't matter. With the tips of his fingers he touched the place under his black coat where he carried a pistol secured in his belt. The long steel barrel felt cold and dangerous against his skin. The man looked about him and then he stepped into the anonymous stream of people. From a safe distance he trailed the others.

Chapter Nine

The irregular cobblestones under their feet, hot from the mid-afternoon sun, burned through the soles of their sandals. Lucio and Corina picked their way along uneasily, like jerking puppets, stepping on their short shadows. Eventually they turned through the maze of shaded, narrow streets and came upon a large, open square at the center of La Paz. The whitewashed walls and the shop windows caught the sunlight and reflected it back into their faces like a polished mirror. The light was so intense that it hurt Lucio's eyes and he had to squint and slit them to find his way.

The chairs along the perimeter of the square were filled with lunchtime tourists who huddled in the little patches of shade under yellow Corona Beer umbrellas, while sipping tall, cold drinks to quench the heat of the afternoon and the fire from the hot salsa. At the center of the square dark skinned children, unattended by adults, splashed in the cool water of a stone fountain. Their laughing shrieks echoed off the walls. Venders with trays full of trinkets wandered from table to table, offering Chiclets for sale and delicate figures carved from sea shells bleached white and hand painted. And an endless procession of beggars made their rounds. Ever optimistic, each individual hoped to catch the ear of the diners with stories that were sad enough to make them part with a handful of *pesos*, or better, some of their American dollars. With the arrival of each new tourist bus in the center of the square, groups of sad faced girls overwhelmed the unsuspecting who had been singled out and cut off from the crowd of shoppers. The youngest and the saddest pressed in much too close with hands extended to accept donations. The older ones, a choreographed distraction of fluttering, colorful fans, became a human screen and afforded the little, expert fingers an opportunity to dip into the unguarded pockets of the smiling, unsuspecting tourists.

The whole time, two *federale* police officers, weighed down by the long barreled pistols they carried in the holsters at their sides, conspired together quietly in a dark corner, taking in the events of another normal afternoon. It was almost time for a little mid-afternoon *siesta*, after they were finished with the free meal provided them each day by the merchants and the shop owners in the square, a reward for their presence and their vigilance. The officers hardly noticed the young Indian man and woman when they came into the square, and they barely looked up from their full plates as Lucio and Corina passed close by them.

Although Corina was hot and tired, she did not want to burden Lucio with her pains. But Lucio seemed to read the thoughts from her mind. "We will rest in there," he said, shading his eyes with one hand and pointing to a small *cantina* at the far end of the square. "It will be cooler. And from there we can watch to see if we have been followed." And as they hurried across the cobblestones and into the *cantina*, Lucio turned to look back over his shoulder.

Inside the *cantina* was thick with patrons at the bar and tourists waiting to be served. The air was filled with the smoke of fried lobsters. These were not the big-clawed lobsters that were taken from the cold waters in the north, but the cheap and tasty, small rock lobsters called *langoustes*. They were a particular favorite of the tourists, who ordered them by the dozens and ate them deep-fried. The pungent smell of hot peppers clung to everything and watered the eyes and the mouths of the diners with the promise of good things to come.

Ignoring those who were waiting to be seated, Lucio and Corina slipped into the empty chairs at a small table in the corner. With his back to the wall as a precaution against surprise, Lucio had an unobstructed view of the street and of the rest of room. Carefully he studied the square through the dirty window. The wavy old glass was marred by a long crack that resembled the coastline of a map or a terrible scar. It ran across the glass and through the faded red and gold lettering that spelled out the owner's name, *Ortéga*. The imperfections in the glass distorted Lucio's view of the outside world when he moved his head to watch the crowded square.

"Soon" he spoke softly, "it will be time for us to separate." And Lucio saw the expression in her eyes change. "You will go back to the village. Stay with your father and mother, where you will be safe. I will continue south toward San José del Cabo, to draw away anyone who might try to follow. Perhaps they will think I plan to sell the pearl there. But I will return in the evening when it is dark. And then I will take my boat and sail north to Loreto or to Santa Rosalita."

When the barman approached them Lucio's body stiffened, as he prepared for another fight. But there was no need, at least for the moment.

The barman took in the two of them at a glance and his assessment was reflected in his haughty attitude and his tone. "What is it that you will have?" he asked gruffly between dark, brown teeth that were clenched around the stub of an equally brown cigar.

"Nothing," Lucio said softly to avoid calling attention to them. "The woman is tired and we will be gone in a moment, after she has rested."

"Perhaps you can not read" the annoyed barman said, and he spit into the sawdust at Lucio's feet. "The sign says this is a *cantina*. And there are customers with money waiting for this table. If it is a rest you want, take the woman into the street-"

"Soon enough," Lucio said with quiet menace in his voice. The look on Lucio's face, the severity of his bruises and the coldness in his eyes stopped the man. "It would be better for everyone," Lucio said, shifting in the chair and revealing the handle of his knife, "if you leave us for a little moment. I have no quarrel with you. We will be gone soon enough."

The man backed away slowly, muttering curses under his breath. He returned to his post behind the bar pouring beer and tequila for the paying customers. But all the time he watched Lucio and Corina. His eyes glared and his cigar stub moved as the man's lips formed silent threats.

Lucio turned to the window and Corina watched his body grow tense from what he saw in the square. "They are coming!" he said.

When she looked, she saw the two men, their faces dark from the sun and from their unshaved beards. They were walking directly toward the *cantina*. Their hands were hidden under their jackets, but Lucio knew that they were armed.

"Lucio, are you sure these are the men?"

"I am sure," he answered. "Quickly!" he hissed at Corina. "Hide yourself. And stay hidden, no matter what happens!" When she hesitated, he snapped at her. "Do as I say, woman! Hide yourself!" And Lucio prepared for what he knew was about to come.

Corina, her eyes dilated with fear, scrambled behind the wooden bar and she hid at the feet of the surprised barman. She tucked herself into a tight ball to make herself small, willing herself to disappear. Her heart was pounding and her breathing was rapid, but she fought hard to regain control of herself. And despite her efforts to remain calm, she jerked involuntarily when she heard the door open with a slam. The sound startled the other patrons at the bar who turned to see who these intruders might be. Then Corina heard Lucio's voice, loud and fierce, but it wasn't words she heard. Rather, it was a sound like the warning snarl of a wild animal. She wanted to look over the bar, to see what was happening, to help Lucio if she could, but she didn't dare to move.

Even before the two surprised men were into the room, Lucio was upon them. And before their eyes could make the adjustment from the intense outside light to the darkness inside the *cantina*, Lucio came at them through their blindness, springing over the table with the fierceness of a mountain lion. His speed and the force of his attack sent all of them sprawling to the sawdust-covered floor. Momentarily, the patrons in the *cantina*, as surprised as the two men, remained motionless, in a silent tableau. When the scene registered fully, some dove for cover behind tables, while others scrambled for safety through the open door and into the street. All was chaos.

Lucio rolled to his feet with his machete ready. He slashed at the first man who had also regained his footing. But Lucio did not use the flat edge as he had done in the church, and the sharp blade of his heavy knife hacked a deep wedge into the man's chest. There was an open mouthed look of surprise on the man's face, as a last gasp of breath escaped from him. Dark blood gurgled from his lips and he died as he stood. With his hand still grasping his own knife, the dead man fell back in a bloody heap, like a marionette whose strings were suddenly broken.

Lucio wheeled on the second man, focusing all of his senses upon him. So intent was he that Lucio didn't hear the panicked shouts from the patrons in the *cantina*. He didn't notice the barman approaching him from behind, wielding a heavy sawed off wooden baseball bat. And Lucio didn't see the two *federale* officers at the door with their guns drawn.

Lucio circled slowly to the right, staring into his pursuer's wide eyes, where he saw the glint of fear. Then Lucio feinted left. When the confused man committed himself and lunged forward with his thin stiletto knife like a dueling foil, his fate was sealed. Lucio pulled back quickly and ended the fight with another sharp stroke from his machete. The blow was quick and hard. It cut off the man's hand cleanly above the wrist, causing the blood to pump from the stump like a fountain. Now nothing could stop Lucio from finishing the job and he raised his machete for the kill. Nothing could stop him but the explosion of a pistol shot that sent a bullet tearing through the tin ceiling of the *cantina*.

"*Manos arriba!*" one of the officers shouted his order. "Hands up!"

At once, the barman dropped his bat that bounced on the wooden floor and rolled in a semi-circle at his feet. Quickly he raised his hands high into the air, shouting at the officers to identify himself, hoping the next shot wasn't through him.

The second officer stepped toward the wounded man, who was jumping and screaming while trying unsuccessfully to staunch the flow of his blood. The officer hit the hysterical man on the back of the head with the butt of his heavy pistol and sent him unconscious to the bloody sawdust.

Lucio turned to run, but all paths of escape were cut off. He was like a trapped animal in the panic of capture. Without thinking, he covered his face and crashed through the cracked window. The glass shattered all around him and rained down like a thousand shining stars in the middle of the sunlit afternoon. A jagged edge sliced his cheek and another opened a deep cut in his thigh. But Lucio felt nothing. He heard the whistle of a bullet flying past his ear like an insect, and then he heard the explosion of the shot, followed by two more shots. Lucio never hesitated, but continued his escape across the square, as the startled tourists drew together and watched. In seconds he was gone.

Amid the shouting and the confusion, Corina crawled from her hiding place behind the bar. She strained to see the two bodies that were down on the bloody floor. She was relieved that neither man was Lucio. She looked at the light flooding in from the open space where the window had once been and through which Lucio had escaped. In her mind she said a silent Hail Mary that he had not been hurt by the bullets and she begged the Holy Virgin for her protection of Lucio and for his continued safety. Then, as the people came out from their hiding places and the shouting voices grew in intensity, she slipped unnoticed through the back door of the *cantina*. By the time the barman remembered where she had been hiding and alerted the two *federales*, Corina was also gone.

She picked her way cautiously through the crowd, moving from group to curious group until she reached the perimeter of the square. Then Corina ran as fast as her legs were able, until she was out of breath, until the stitch in her side forced her to stop and rest. But her concern was only for Lucio. She made up her mind that she would go to his boat and not back to her house, as Lucio had instructed her. There, she thought, she would wait for him to return in the night as he had said he would. Then, no matter how much he objected, she would sail with him wherever he went. And when they were safely away from La Paz, he could sell his pearl or throw it away for all she cared. No matter. She would become his wife and they would be together for life. On this she would insist.

Corina looked back to see if she was being followed by the *federales*, but there was no sign of anyone. She had not seen the scar-faced man who had witnessed everything and who waited patiently in the shadows to make his move. She was unaware. And when Corina moved again, the scar-faced man went with her and followed her at a distance.

Chapter Ten

In the evening a sudden storm blew up unexpectedly out of the Sea of Cortez. The ominous clouds, threatening to pour down rain, blotted out the almost full moon and darkened the sky. A strong wind whipped through La Paz. It toppled the yellow Corona Beer umbrellas in the square and upturned the restaurant tables. It scattered the tourists who were still out for a late night on the town, and they ran back to the security of their hotels. The braver souls, who were determined that nothing would interrupt their celebrations, or those, fortified by tequila who were more foolish, waited out the storm in the *cantinas*, against whatever might happen.

The wind roared through the village with the sound of a freight train. It drove the coarse sand through the air like needles that stung anyone who had the misfortune to be out in such a night. Birds huddled together under the protection of their wings, fighting to keep perched on tree branches, or to safeguard in fragile nests their clutches of hatchlings. Stray dogs and the domestic pigs shared hiding places in the dark spaces under the huts. Frantic and frightened hens in their roosts cackled and squawked in anticipation of what they knew was to come, while fearless roosters strutted brazenly and sounded their defiant challenge to the approaching storm.

Even the fish out in the estuary sensed the impending danger. As with the land creatures, which realized that their security and survival often depended on banding together in large numbers, so the little fish, driven by the growing storm, formed large schools for their protection. Ironically, the sharks and the other predators also came into the estuary to gorge themselves in the teeming waters close to the shore. They made the estuary churn and boil in a struggle of life and death.

Inside their frail houses the people were no strangers to the whims of Nature. Calmly they sniffed the salty night air and they recalled the many times within their own lifetimes when fierce winds had leveled the village and reduced everything to debris. They, too, banded together in their homes for protection. And since there was nothing they could do to prevent the inevitable, they were fatalistic in their hearts and they waited patiently for whatever God or Fate would send at them. They knew that those who survived would bury the dead, rebuild from the ruins, like the mythical Phoenix, and get on with their lives.

Lucio was exhausted and he was in a great deal of pain when he finally reached his boat. He had spent the long afternoon hiding, from the *federales*, who had joined the search after him for murder in the *cantina* and from anyone else who still might have an interest in his pearl. The wind driven sand got into his eyes and his mouth, choking him, and it stung in his open wounds. Sharp twigs and branches added to his pain, so that Lucio could feel the places where the glass had cut him again weeping blood.

A part of him was relieved. The storm would cover up his trail. And though it would make his journey north in his boat more difficult and more perilous, it would also prevent him from being followed. Lucio was a confident and experienced sailor. He had been out in high seas and strong winds many times before and he knew that these unexpected winds would carry him more quickly along the coast to his destination.

Into the bottom of the boat Lucio dropped the bottle of fresh water and the sack of hard biscuits that he had collected along the way for his journey. Then he stepped the short mast with the furled sail still attached, bracing it against the wind with his sore shoulder. Once he was away from the shore and his lines were set, he would release the canvas and the wind filled sail would take him to safety. With any luck he would be in Loreto before it was light and then many of his troubles would be over.

Lucio laid his chest against the boat and he pushed with whatever strength he had left. The pressure of the wooden prow against his bruised body made him wince, but Lucio struggled against his pain. Slowly and steadily he inched the beached boat along the sand and the seashells, stopping when he needed to regain some of his strength. It was a long and hard ordeal and Lucio was relieved when the stern finally began to float in the eddy of water near the breakers. He was about to jump aboard, when a cold, menacing voice called out of the darkness.

"That will be far enough."

Lucio reached for his machete in his belt, as two shadowy figures approached.

Clouds, like dumplings, skated across the surprised face of the full moon, and the light and dark danced eerily together over the water and the land. When the moon again peered from behind the clouds, Lucio saw that one of the shadows was Corina. The other was a scar-faced man that Lucio didn't recognize, but he knew why he was there. The two moved closer and Lucio saw the glint of light reflecting from the long barrel of the man's pistol.

"Corina," Lucio called to her, "are you all right?"

But she didn't answer. There was great fear in her face and tears in corners of Corina's dark eyes that were two small reflected moons.

Lucio spoke to the man. "What do you want with me?" he asked, hoping that the man might be a *federale* who had come to arrest him. But Lucio knew better and he knew there was nothing he could do now to escape.

"This is not the time for games. You know what I want," the man said. His words were harsh and dry. He edged Corina forward, at the same time he tightened his grip around her wrist that was twisted behind her back. The man pressed the end of the gun barrel against her neck. "The pearl," he said. "Hand it over. And maybe I will let the two of you live."

Now there was a distance of only some yards between them. In his mind Lucio calculated the space and the fraction of a second it would take him to swing his heavy blade against this man's head. But there was also Corina. And Lucio knew this man with the scarred face and the cruel eyes wouldn't hesitate to pull the trigger. Even if Lucio managed to kill the man before he fired a second bullet, he knew that the first would tear through Corina, and she would be dead before she hit the ground. Had he been facing this man alone, Lucio would not have hesitated. He would have taken the chance, trusting to his luck, to God, that he might move faster than the bullet. But he couldn't gamble with the life of Corina.

The water surged around Lucio's feet. His boat, anxious to be out to sea, nudged Lucio's back as a horse eager for a gallop might nuzzle its master for a gentle touch. Lucio dropped his machete and he reached slowly under his shirt for the pearl.

When the man saw its size and its perfect beauty, he wasn't prepared. His eyes opened in wide surprise and his mouth gaped open in a stunned smiled. "Such a pearl," he said, "could easily tempt a man to forget any agreement he may have made and cause him to set out on his own." He snatched the pearl from Lucio's hand. "Now," he commanded Corina, "get into the boat." He pushed her forward and she stumbled into Lucio's arms.

"Wait," Lucio said. "You have the pearl. You are a rich man. Take it and let us go." He saw that the man wasn't moved. "At least the girl."

The man leveled the barrel and aimed it directly at Lucio's heart. "Both of you into the boat," he said. "The girl first."

Reluctantly Lucio helped her aboard.

"You," he said to Lucio and motioned with his pistol, "step back and push us off from the shore. Then, when the boat is away, you get in. And no tricks, or you know I will kill her." He turned the gun on Corina.

As the man stepped over the side, his weight caused the boat to dip and he had to steady himself with both hands to keep from falling. It was Lucio's chance, maybe the only opportunity he would have to try and save them. But he hesitated and let the moment pass.

"You are smart," the man said, as though he had read Lucio's thoughts, "not to try. This girl is no matter to me, alive or dead. And neither are you."

Lucio braced himself against the high prow to turn the boat in the water. And when they had broken free from the sand, Lucio deftly boarded. He took the tiller and cradled it under his arm. He pulled on the frayed line with his free hand, allowing the furled sail to open. It filled with the gusting wind and the old boat cut silently and swiftly through the curling breakers.

"Directly ahead," the man ordered gruffly. He held Lucio's pearl tightly in one hand and he gripped his pistol with relaxed familiarity in the other.

Corina moved closer to Lucio in the stern and she took hold of his hand. She was shivering with cold and with her fear. "Lucio," she whispered, "he is going to kill us both."

"I will find a way," he whispered back to try and allay her fears. But Lucio realized the desperate situation that they faced.

"Don't worry," the man said, " I am a kind man. I will make it quick. And the both of you will be dead before you go into the water. The sharks will make short work of the clean up. But you won't feel anything." He smiled and he studied the pearl that he held in his right hand, considering the options that it made possible for him. He braced himself as the boat continued over the swells, and after a short silence he spoke again. "This is far enough." And he stood up in the rocking boat. "On your feet," he ordered.

Lucio could hear Corina crying behind him. He had hoped that something might save them, but now their time had run out and he was desperate. If he could distract the man, Lucio thought, and cause the boat to capsize in the waves, they might have one last chance. But in his heart he knew it was too late.

"I am sorry," Lucio whispered to her, "that I have brought you to this." He hoped that he would be the first and not have to watch Corina die. He heard the man cock the hammer of his pistol. And with a quick prayer of contrition for all his sins, Lucio prepared himself to die. When the clouds uncovered the moon, a ray of light fell across the boat and Lucio, in the final second of his life, could see everything, his life and death, in crystal clarity. Everything was so clear to him now.

Then, off to the right something dark moved into Lucio's peripheral vision. At the same time that Lucio became aware of the movement, he heard a sound that he recognized as the hiss of a speeding boat slicing through the water. Immediately the dark form emerged from the shadows and rammed into the middle of Lucio's boat like a torpedo. The high prow of this phantom craft crushed the painted wood into splinters and continued forward, bringing down the mast and sail. The boat came to a standstill and there it remained, attached.

Corina screamed. The force of the impact knocked Lucio off his feet and brought him to his knees. The unexpected collision turned the startled scar-faced man and his finger jerked on the trigger. The pistol fired with a loud crack that was carried by the wind across the water, like the clap of thunder. But the sudden impact changed the path of the bullet that was intended for Lucio. And all of this happened so quickly. But to Lucio it was just like the time he was a child at the movie house in La Paz watching the people on the screen in slow motion.

Granted a momentary reprieve from death, Lucio sprang into action. Bracing against the pitching boat to regain his balance, he leaped at the surprised man. With both of his hands Lucio grabbed for the pistol, and in their desperate struggle two more shots were fired. The barrel of the gun was so close to Lucio's face that the flash from the exploding powder burned him and he was blinded for a second. But Lucio only tightened his grip on the man's hand and he pressed his attack. The two boats, joined at the center like a pair of violent lovers, rocked perversely in the darkness.

Suddenly all around them the water churned in a frenzy of fish that boiled up through the surface. It was as if these little fish had a stake in the outcome of the strange events occurring in the alien world above them and had come to witness the outcome. But just below the boats, another life and death struggle was being enacted, as the large predators again came in to feed.

Directly above the struggling fish, the scar-faced man was no match for the wild animal strength that was in Lucio. Unwilling to lose possession of the pearl, the man momentarily relaxed his hold on the pistol and it fell from his numb hand, clattering into the bottom of the boat that was now taking on water. Realizing that the man was disarmed, Lucio now turned all of his attention and his remaining strength to the recover his pearl. Expending every ounce of energy that was left in him, Lucio slowly peeled back first one finger and then another and seemed about to wrestle the precious pearl from the man's grasp. But even in this extremity the scar-faced man would not concede. With his free hand he slowly reached inside his pocket and removed a long slender knife that he flicked open with a snap of his wrist. The blade flashed in the moonlight and he stabbed at Lucio once, twice in the side. The sharp, burning pain took away Lucio's breath.

Lucio relinquished his grip, letting go of the man's hand and the pearl, and he vainly tried to stem the flow of blood with his fingers. This advantage was all the man needed and he moved in for the kill. His knife was in motion. Lucio closed his eyes that were stinging from the salt and sweat and he prepared for a second time to meet Death. But a loud explosion stopped the man cold. The force of a single bullet tore through the man's chest and it propelled him over the side into the wild water.

At the same instant Lucio made a desperate lunge for him, for the pearl that he still held. But Lucio was too slow and the man landed with a loud splash. All Lucio could do was watch helplessly as the triangular dorsal fins cut through the dark water toward the surprised man who was holding his bloody chest. For a second the water boiled red as the sharks dragged the scar-faced man toward the bottom. And with him went Lucio's "Pearl of the World."

From behind him Lucio heard a distant voice, as if he were waking from a bad dream. It was Corina. "Papa! Papa!" she sobbed.

Lucio turned to see Ernesto with his head cradled in Corina's arms and the scar-faced man's pistol in his hand. It was Ernesto who had fired the shot that saved Lucio's life. But now the old man lay dying in the bottom of the boat covered with his own blood, wounded by one stray bullet that had found him in the darkness.

"Ernesto," Lucio said, " you are shot."

"It does not matter, Lucio," he answered weakly. "I came," he said haltingly, "to save my daughter. To help you, Lucio. And to make amends." His eyes were wet with tears. He knew that he was dying and he desperately wanted to make his last confession, to make his peace before it was too late. "Can you–" He paused from the pain and from the shame that he felt. "–can you forgive a foolish old man – for what he has done to you?" Corina rocked her father's head and her tears spilled down her cheeks. "It was I who came to your house that first night – with Clementé."

Although he heard Ernesto's words Lucio didn't need to be told. In his mind he had pieced it all together, everything except the reason for such actions. And he was still confused. "Why, Ernesto?" Lucio asked. "Did you think that I would not share my good fortune with you, the father of my wife, my only family?"

"I am so – ashamed," Ernesto said. "I acted out of envy – out of greed – out of my own stupidity. And for that – poor Clementé–" He took a deep breath that gurgled in his chest and his voice was weaker when he was finally able to speak. "I have prayed – and asked for God's forgiveness. But can *you* ever forgive me, Lucio?"

Lucio leaned forward and he embraced his friend. The blood from his wounds mingled with that of the old man's. "Of course I forgive you, Ernesto, my father."

"Thank you, Lucio. My son. That is all that I can ask of you." The old man smiled and nodded. "Don't cry, Corina," he said to his sobbing daughter. "Tell your mother that my last thought was of her." Then Ernesto's eyes closed.

When they were able, Corina and Lucio separated the two boats. Together, through their tears, they witnessed another death, as Ernesto's craft foundered and dipped below the calming surface of the water.

Out in the Gulf the storm subsided and the bright moon pinned against the sky lit a path toward home. Sitting in silence close together, Lucio and Corina sailed the damaged boat back to shore. In the morning they would tell their story to the village, of the loss of Lucio's perfect pearl, and how Ernesto had sacrificed his life unselfishly to save his children. And then they would make their arrangements – for Ernesto's funeral, and for their wedding.

The feeding frenzy was over and the little fish went on with living, as all of La Paz prepared for another day. And on the rocky bottom of the sea, that which remained of a man's hand still clung to the great pearl.

The End